unnamed

unnamed

N. THEISS

Paperback ISBN: 979-8-9907745-1-3
eBook ISBN: 979-8-9907745-3-7

Edited by HEA Author Services
Formatting and interior design by Joanne Martin
Cover design by GetCovers

To the survivors who endured the unthinkable.
To those still trapped, fighting invisible battles.
To those who never made it out.

This book is yours—

A name for the nameless,
A voice for the voiceless,
A flame to burn through the darkness of hell.

reader beware

This is NOT a sweet romance.
It's not a romance at all.
There's nothing romantic about it.

If you're looking for a strong hero to whisk our heroine away and save her, this book is not for you. If you're looking for a villain's redemption arc, this book is not for you. But…if you're looking for a story about a heroine who, under the most dire, extreme, and harrowing circumstances, takes matters into her own hands and saves herself, then you've picked up the right book.

This is a **brutally dark piece of erotic fiction**. (See, "romance" was nowhere in that description.) It is extremely graphic, unhinged, and depraved. When I started writing it, I never intended for it to see the light of day. But something inside is telling me that this story needs to be told—to be a voice for people who have no voice and no name.

I'm not typically a fan of trigger warning lists, but I feel compelled to list a few so that you can make an informed decision on whether or not to proceed with this book.

- Non-consent/dubious consent
- Sexual assault
- Human trafficking
- Bondage
- Anal play
- Forced drug use
- Examination
- Gangbang
- Training/grooming
- Physical and psychological abuse
- Humiliation and degradation
- Death on the page (not the protagonist)

Still with me?

Ah, you're as depraved as I am then. We're going to get along just fine.

show

. . .

"YOU KNOW THE RULES. You can look, touch, tongue, whatever—just keep your dick in your pants. No marks, permanent damage, or excessive abuse of the product. If you choose to purchase after your trial, I'll organize the transfer once we receive the full sale price via wire. If you do any serious damage to the product, you'll be charged double the sale price. You break it, you buy it. And, it goes without saying, but if you violate any of our rules, you'll be permanently banned."

He sounded like a robot, like he had gone through this script a thousand times. He probably had.

"Yeah, yeah, I know the drill."

I couldn't see the second man, but from his voice, I imagined him old and gruff with chubby, clumsy hands.

My arms burned from being restrained over my head. The chain was taut, and even on tiptoes, I could barely touch the damp concrete floor.

"Your time starts when I leave the room. You have thirty minutes."

"Then make tracks." His voice was throaty. "I'm getting impatient here."

The metal door hinges groaned, followed by the heavy clank of a lock. Footsteps thudded toward me. My heart raced, and my gut squirmed, but outwardly, I stayed silent and calm. This would be over in thirty minutes.

"Well, aren't you a pretty one," he said, almost admiringly. "Though I hate that you're already naked. Unwrapping the package is half the fun."

This wasn't my first trial. I knew how to detach, how to make my mind float above my body, observing from a safe distance. These men all wanted the same thing—a reaction. Fear, trembling, resistance, feistiness, *something*. I gave them nothing.

"What's your name?"

"Jade," I replied automatically.

"No, no, no. I know they name you here like dogs at the shelter. What's your real name?"

"Jade," I repeated. My real name was the only thing I had left that was mine.

He let out a grunt but didn't press the question further. "Well, *Jade*…let's get rid of this blindfold. I want to see those pretty blue eyes for myself."

Clumsy fingers fumbled roughly at the knot behind my head. The fabric loosened and fell away, leaving me momentarily blinded by the stark fluorescent lighting. I blinked hard, my vision slowly sharpening to reveal a man —probably in his fifties—in a pinstriped suit. His voice made him sound older, probably from late nights and too much whiskey. He'd slicked back his silver-streaked hair. His chest was broader and more muscular than I had expected. In any other circumstance, he might have been considered attractive.

He looked me up and down slowly. His eyes lingered on my chest.

"Your info sheet said you were tall and blonde with natural D cups," he muttered. "Had to see it to believe it."

He reached out and palmed one of my breasts, squeezing like he was testing the ripeness of fruit.

"Hmm." He grunted. "Nice and firm. For once, they're accurate." He circled to stand behind me, pressing his body into my back. He reached around me and palmed both breasts, kneading them roughly.

There was a bed in the corner of the room—luxurious-looking compared to everything else—with thick red linens that seemed absurdly plush for such a stark setting. The rest of the room was pure concrete—walls, floor, even the ceiling had a bunker-like feel, except for small ventilation slats near where the wall met the roofline.

He grabbed a fistful of my hair and pulled back. My shoulders screamed in their sockets. "I usually prefer brunettes," he said, his breath hot against my ear. "But there's something about your look that just screams classic." He slid his free hand down the flat of my stomach. "I'd ask if the carpet matches the drapes, but you're shaved smooth—just how I like it."

My body involuntarily jolted as he parted me and grazed a grubby finger over my clit.

"Let's see how you warm up." He rolled my clit around in circles under his finger.

I struggled to stay stoic, but he was unrelenting.

"I'm going to make this pussy purr."

He unhooked me from the chain, and I almost

collapsed. Blood rushed back into my arms, a thousand needles pricking at once. I tried to suppress a groan of relief but couldn't hold it in.

"Lie down on the bed," he said, stepping back with an imperious wave of his hand. "Let me get a better look at what I'm paying for."

I walked slowly to the bed, every muscle sore and stiff from the prolonged tension. Too slow for him, apparently. He shoved me forward, and I stumbled and fell face-first onto the bed.

"Trying to play down the clock?"

I said nothing in response. My only reprieve was that the sheets were sumptuously soft and silky smooth.

He shrugged out of his jacket, loosened his tie, and rolled up the sleeves of his dress shirt. "Lie on your back," he commanded.

I did as he said, lying flat on my back with my arms at my sides.

"Now hug your knees to your chest and let those legs fall open wide."

I again did as he said, this time with the lingering dull ache in my limbs from being chained for so long.

"Look at that." He leered, running a finger along the inside of one thigh, stopping short of touching me where I knew he wanted to. He licked his lips. "Such a perfect little cunt." He knelt down for a closer look, his hot breath wafting over me. "Not even wet yet?" He clicked his tongue. "We'll have to do something about that."

He spread me with his fingers, stretching the delicate skin almost to the point of tearing. Pain shot through me.

"I love how your pink is just peeking out." He admired

his work with a sick fascination. "A fucking five-course meal on display just for me."

He moved closer, and I braced for what I knew was coming. His tongue flicked out and lapped at me like a dog drinking water—quick strokes that sent unwanted electric shocks through me.

"You taste as good as you look," he said, saliva glistening on his lips. He dove back in with renewed vigor, sucking and slurping and groaning with obscene enthusiasm. My hands gripped the sheets in unconscious tension, knuckles white as bone. His head bobbed between my legs as he worked me over—a grotesque parody of worship. Every few seconds, he'd pause to deliver another comment—on my flavor, on how he was already imagining owning me, on the myriad ways he'd enjoy me once I was his.

I stared at the concrete ceiling, counting the small cracks and imperfections. *Thirty minutes. Just thirty minutes.*

He inserted a finger, and my body betrayed me by clenching against my will.

"There it is," he said with a sick triumph. "Getting nice and warm." He added another finger, carefully watching my face as he stretched me, pumping in and out with a methodical, unhurried rhythm.

"So tight around just two fingers. Imagine how you'd squeeze a cock."

I refused to look at him, biting the inside of my cheek hard enough to draw blood, letting that pain distract me from what he was doing below.

"You know," he said, not breaking his disgusting tempo, "most girls are soaking by now. You're making this difficult." He curved his fingers upward inside me, seeking the sensitive spot that made most women melt. I willed myself into stone.

Filthy words poured from him as he described every obscene detail—how he'd ruin me if given the chance, how he'd stretch me open like an overused toy, how no man could resist owning something as perfect as I was supposed to be. Each stroke of his hand came with another burst of degrading yet oddly clinical commentary.

"Look at your little hole gripping me for dear life," he sneered. "You're starting to dribble down my hand." His tone dripped with ego.

He withdrew his fingers slowly and held them up to my face so I could see their slickness under the harsh light. He wiped his fingers clean on my breasts.

"But wet isn't good enough. I want you absolutely dripping."

He reached into his pocket and fished out a small silver vibrator.

Shit.

"You're holding back on me, I know it." He clicked on the vibrator and pressed it to my nipple. "Trying to stay all stoic and serene." He moved the vibrator to my other nipple. "But we both know you're just a filthy whore who can't get enough."

He held the vibrator to my pubic bone, letting the vibrations travel downward. My body had a mind of its own. Despite my best efforts to remain detached, I was starting to involuntarily respond.

"There we go," he said, his tone pleased. "Be a good little slut and moan for me."

I clamped my lips together.

He slid the vibrator down and pressed it against my

clit. A gasp escaped me before I could choke it back. He held the vibrator there, applying just enough pressure to be maddening.

"You like that?" he asked, though he didn't care about the answer. "Your pretty little slit looks so needy." He adjusted the angle, letting the vibrator roll over my clit in slow circles. My hips started to betray me, tilting upward to meet each pass.

"You can't hide how much you want it," he said. "I can see your body begging for release." His words were a running commentary of every obscene thought that crossed his mind. "If only you could see yourself right now —legs spread wide like a whore, panting, begging for my cock…"

My chest rose and fell with deep breaths as I fought for control. But the sensations were overpowering—no amount of mental detachment could fully block them out.

He increased the pressure on my clit, holding it steady as my body tensed and twitched against its will. "Come on," he urged. "Let go, and show me how much you enjoy this."

I bit down harder on the inside of my cheek, tasting coppery blood, but it wasn't enough to drown out what was happening below.

"If you come for me like a good girl, I'll go ahead and purchase you."

Anything but that.

He moved the vibrator away for just a moment, and my body sagged with relief. It was short-lived.

"Like that? I can see you do." He smirked as he pushed two fingers back inside me in one hard thrust while pressing the vibrator against my clit again. His movements were infuriatingly precise, hitting every nerve ending like he'd memorized an anatomical map of pleasure.

"I knew it—you're nothing but a slutty little toy," he said with breathless excitement. "Look how your greedy cunt swallows my fingers." He began pistoning his fingers in and out, adding slick sounds to his symphony of degradation. "You're gonna come all over my hand, aren't you?"

I shook my head but stayed silent. He intensified the pressure of the vibrator while curling his fingers inside me, hitting a spot that drew an unwilling shudder from deep within me.

"Yes, yes—there we fucking go," he exclaimed with triumphant zeal. "Look at your body squirming for it." His grin widened as his tempo increased. I could feel the burn and stretch in my muscles anew.

"Your little pussy is going to make such a delicious mess when you finally fucking let go."

He was relentless with every thrust inside me and every circle of my clit.

My thighs trembled, and white pinpricks of light dotted my vision.

"Just imagine it's my cock making you come," he said with a sick sort of encouragement, his voice full of explosive ego. "You're going to burst all over like you're meant to."

The tension built beyond what I could endure, and every muscle contracted as an unwelcome wave started cresting inside me.

"That's it," he breathed. "I can feel you squeezing me like you're about to burst." His eyes gleamed with sadistic pleasure. "Come for me, you tight little cunt."

The waves crashed over me despite every ounce of resistance I could muster. My back arched off the bed as a guttural moan tore free from my throat, raw and animalistic. It was my voice, but I didn't recognize it.

"Yes! Fucking yes!" he shouted, his fingers persisting in their assault even as I convulsed around them. The vibrator, held firm against my clit, sent shockwaves through my already overloaded system.

"You're gushing like fucking Niagara Falls," he said with perverse admiration mixed into his derision. He withdrew his fingers and rubbed the slickness between them.

A hot stream of fluid flooded out of me and onto the sheets.

After the final shockwave subsided, he clicked off the vibrator.

My body lay in a defeated heap, chest heaving.

"Get on your hands and knees," he commanded.

I started to comply but didn't move fast enough for him. He yanked me by the arm until I was in position, teetering unsteadily on all fours. I could barely breathe, still caught up in the intense aftermath of what had just been forced upon me.

"Look at the mess you made. Lap it up."

He shoved my face into the damp sheet. I hesitated for just one second before a sharp pain twisted at the back of my neck as his hand held my head down.

"Lick your filth off of these goddamn sheets." He moved my hair so he could see.

I screwed up my face and blinked back tears. I knew as soon as the dam broke, there'd be no stopping the deluge, and it would give this bastard exactly what he wanted.

I slid my tongue along the smooth satin of the red sheet, lapping up the traitorous fluid that had betrayed my body.

He loosened his grip on my neck, and I lifted my head slowly.

"Good girl," he purred, rubbing the back of my head as if I were a pet.

He positioned me on my hands and knees, and when I was situated to his satisfaction, he massaged my swinging breasts. He slid his hands down my torso to my hips.

"There we go. Right where you're supposed to be," he said, gripping my ass with both hands and squeezing hard enough to leave bruises. His fingers dug into my flesh as if staking a claim before pulling my ass cheeks apart in slow motion, spreading me wide open for his inspection.

"Fuck yes…look at this pretty little hole." He exhaled sharply, like he'd discovered some treasure. "So fucking tight. I bet you'll make all sorts of wonderful noises once I'm inside your ass," he mused aloud while running one thumb along my crease without any tenderness whatsoever —just calculated focus on exposing everything private about me to him.

Leather and metal slid as he unbuckled his belt, and fabric rustled as he dropped his pants before a voice crackled over the intercom.

"Remember the rules. Keep your dick in your pants."

"I know the rules," he said with a hint of annoyance. "I just don't want to stain my slacks."

My heart pounded with equal parts of fear and relief.

"You've got ten minutes left in your trial," crackled the dispassionate voice from above.

I risked a glance back at the man who was carefully

draping his slacks over the back of a chair. I caught him pulling something from the pocket—a shiny black silicone butt plug. My stomach clenched, but I stayed perfectly still.

He held up the butt plug so I could see it clearly, then brought it closer to my face. "Open your mouth," he ordered.

When I hesitated too long for his liking, he squeezed my jaw until it popped open painfully.

"Suck on it like it's my cock."

The taste was neutral, but knowing where it was destined to go made me gag around its thickness as he shoved it deeper than necessary into my mouth.

"That's it," he said, twisting the plug in my mouth. "Get it nice and wet for your pretty little asshole."

He popped the toy from my mouth before moving behind me. The blunt tip of the butt plug pressed against my ass.

"Relax," he sneered as I clenched reflexively, anticipating the pain that was bound to follow.

The cold silicone prodded harder, and I braced every inch of my body. I knew resistance would only make it worse, but I couldn't help it. A sharp intake of breath, a moment of searing pain, and then a dull, invasive ache as he wedged the plug inside me.

"There," he pronounced with satisfaction, like an artist stepping back from his latest piece. "Now you look perfect."

I closed my eyes and tried to dissociate, imagining myself floating above the room, detached from the puppet-me below that was forced to endure his whims. But his voice yanked me back to earth.

"Don't think we're done," he said, circling to where I

could see his erect cock straining against his boxers. He stroked it deliberately, leisurely, letting me take in every crude detail.

He sat on the wooden chair and gestured for me to move toward him.

"Crawl to me, and come sit on my lap."

I complied slowly, every movement a struggle as I crawled over to him like a wounded animal. He grabbed my hips and pulled me onto his lap.

"That's it. Straddle me, sweetheart."

I wrapped my legs around his waist as he asked. The hard contour of the butt plug made me wince as it pressed in deeper from the weight of my own body.

His eyes and hands roamed freely over my skin, claiming every inch as he pleased. I stared at the wall behind him, focusing on the bland gray paint and the tiny crack that ran diagonally from the corner of the ceiling toward the floor.

He squeezed my breasts roughly. "There we go," he murmured with obscene delight blooming in his eyes as he kneaded the pliant flesh like a potter working clay. "You've got such beautiful tits."

He pinched both nipples hard enough to make me gasp, rolling them between his thumb and forefinger. He drank in every little twitch I couldn't suppress, watching intently while expertly manipulating those sensitive peaks, and they hardened traitorously under his rough attention.

"Fuck yes…love seeing your tits perk up for me." His voice had taken on an animalistic growl, vibrating with lustful hunger undiluted by restraint or shame. He bounced my breasts up and down in his hands, testing the weight. "Look at these fucking huge tits, just begging to be sucked."

He latched his mouth onto my left breast, sucking hard like a starving infant. A jolt of sensation shot through me as his tongue flicked and swirled around my nipple. He bit down lightly, then harder, sending threads of pain and unwelcome pleasure shooting through my chest.

He switched to the other breast with ravenous fervor. "So fucking perfect," he mumbled around his mouthful of my flesh. His saliva cooled in the open air as he suckled and gnawed like an animal marking its territory.

"Grind your pussy on me," he said between sucks, one hand creeping down to grope my ass again while the other crushed my breast against his face.

I started to move my hips against him in slow circles, the hard length of his cock pressing against me through the thin fabric of his boxers. The butt plug shifted uncomfortably inside me with each motion, sending unwelcome sparks up my spine.

"That's it," he mumbled through a mouthful of breast. "Rub that wet cunt all over me." He released my nipple with a pop and looked up at me. Sweat had formed along his hairline from exertion or excitement—maybe both.

He slid his hands down my back and gripped my hips again as I straddled him. "You know," he said, almost thoughtfully, "it's so fucking tempting to break the rules and sink into you right now." He thrust his pelvis upward once to emphasize the point, making me feel every inch of his erection through the fabric barrier. "But I know how this works."

Relief washed over me again, then was immediately

crushed by the sick knowledge that this was only a temporary reprieve.

He grabbed my hair and pulled my face close to his. "Besides," he whispered harshly, "I'm going to buy you anyway. So there's no point in doubling your price and getting banned."

He reached around and tapped on the butt plug.

I couldn't contain my shocked yelp.

"When you're mine, I'm going to fill every hole you've got and stuff you like a Christmas turkey." He tweaked the butt plug again. "Wouldn't you like that, baby?"

I kept my eyes trained on the wall. Darkness seeped into the corners of my vision, threatening to swallow me whole.

"I fucking said grind." He gripped my hips and forcefully rocked me back and forth on his lap. "We only have a few minutes left, and I want to get my money's worth."

I moved as he commanded, grinding my pelvis against him with mechanical obedience. Each stroke set the butt plug shifting inside me, a cruel reminder of his control and my complete lack of it.

"That's better," he groaned, tilting his head back in pleasure. "Feel how fucking hard you make me?" He groaned again, his cock pulsing and throbbing beneath me. "I can't wait to sink my cock into your tight little cunt."

"Time's up," crackled the voice from above. My heart leaped, though I knew better than to let hope show on my face.

The man beneath me let out a frustrated sigh and pushed me off his lap. I stood unsteadily, my legs weak and wobbly like a newborn foal's. He didn't rush as he adjusted his boxers and retrieved his slacks from the back of the chair. He took his time dressing, savoring each moment as if it were a fine wine.

"I'll see you soon, baby," he said, smirking as he walked to the door. "I'm going to take care of your paperwork, and you'll be in my bed by dinnertime."

I stood there. Motionless. Silent.

"And keep that plug in. I have big plans for that tight little asshole, and I want you nice and ready for me."

submit

. . .

"YOU WILL EAT, sleep, shower, and fuck. That's it."

I nodded, keeping my gaze trained on the bright geometric patterns on the plush carpet. My knees ached from kneeling on the floor, and my ass burned from the plug.

"Your job is to fuck. Whenever I want, however I want, and—from time to time—whomever I want. You've got to earn everything, and you earn it by fucking. You want to eat? You've got to fuck for it. You want to sleep? You've got to earn that too. Do you understand?"

He gripped me by the chin and forced me to look up at him. "I just paid a shit ton of money for you. The least you can do is fucking answer me."

I swallowed hard, the dryness in my throat making it feel like sandpaper. "I understand."

The man—my new owner—smiled. It was a predatory thing, all teeth and no warmth. "You will stay naked, clean, and shaven at all times. The only place I want hair is on your head. You will serve me whenever and however I choose. And you will perform with vigor and enthusiasm. That dead-fish act you put on during your trial will get you beat faster than you can blink, and you can forget about eating. Got it?"

I nodded.

"Got it?"

"Yes, sir."

"Better." He released my chin, and I let my head drop back down.

"Now that the pleasantries are out of the way, let's pick up where we left off. I've been aching to sink my dick into you and fuck you so hard I split you in half."

The weight of his words crushed me, each syllable a hammer strike to my fragile psyche. I braced myself for what was to come, the tension in my body winding tighter and tighter, like a spring about to snap.

"Don't look so scared," he said, almost laughing. "I'm not a monster. You'll get used to it. Hopefully, you'll even come to enjoy it."

He unbuckled his belt with deliberate slowness, drawing out the moment. The leather slid through the loops of his pants with a soft hiss, and he doubled it over in his hand, testing its flexibility.

"Stand up."

I rose on shaky legs, my whole body quivering like a leaf in a storm. He walked around me in a slow circle, the belt swaying casually in his grip. His eyes carved into my skin, assessing his new property.

"Turn around."

I did as he commanded, my mind retreating to that safe place it had created for moments like this. It was a colorless void where time didn't exist—a place where I could watch events unfold without truly feeling them.

"Hands on the wall."

I placed my palms against the smooth surface before me and closed my eyes. The first strike came swiftly, unexpected, the sharp crack echoing through the room like a gunshot. Pain blossomed across my back, hot and immediate. I bit down hard on my lip to keep from crying out, tasting the metallic tang of blood.

"That's for being a tease," he said, his voice thick with something approaching enjoyment. "Don't think I've forgotten how you held back during the trial."

Another strike, this time lower, that caught the backs of my thighs. My knees buckled, but I forced myself to stay upright, gripping the wall as if it were the only thing keeping me from falling into an abyss.

"And this," he said, pausing for effect, "is just because I can."

The belt whistled through the air and landed with a cruel thud against my buttocks. The impact jolted the butt plug inside me, sending a wave of nauseating discomfort up my spine. Tears pricked at the corners of my eyes, but I willed them not to fall. Showing pain was one thing. Showing weakness was another.

He stepped closer, his breath warm on my ear. "Are you going to be a good investment?" He ran a hand down my welted back, tracing the lines his strikes had left. The touch was almost tender, a grotesque parody of affection.

When I didn't answer him, he growled. "The silence is cute," he said, pulling away, "but not very smart."

The belt whistled through the air and struck my flesh with a vicious snap.

I gasped, the sound escaping before I could clamp it down. The pain was a white-hot streak, like lightning splitting a tree. My vision blurred, and for a moment, I thought I might pass out.

"Are you going to be a good investment?" he repeated.

"Yes, sir," I whimpered.

"That's more like it," he said, satisfaction dripping from his words. "I like to hear what I'm paying for."

He tossed the belt onto a nearby chair with a casual flick of his wrist. My skin tingled, hypersensitive where the leather had kissed it. I clung to the wall, afraid that if I moved even an inch, my body would dissolve into a puddle of anguish.

"Turn around," he commanded.

I sucked in a breath, then turned around gingerly, each movement a ripple of agony through my welted back and thighs. My new owner's eyes gleamed with satisfaction as he drank in the sight of me—helpless, punished, and obedient.

"Get on the bed," he said. It was less a command than an inevitability at this point.

I walked on trembling legs to the four-poster bed dominating one side of the room. I climbed onto it and lay down, the silk sheets cool against my flushed skin. Before I could settle into any position, his hands were already grabbing at my wrists and ankles.

"I'm going to break you in right," he murmured, more to himself than me, as he fetched lengths of rope from beneath the bed frame.

He worked quickly but methodically, securing my wrists before spreading out my legs and tying each ankle. I was flat on my back, splayed open wide for him.

"You look fucking delicious all tied up like this." He dropped his slacks and boxers in a pool on the floor and unbuttoned his shirt.

The man stood naked, chest puffed out with the arrogance of a conqueror surveying his spoils. He stroked himself lazily, eyes never leaving my body. The anticipation was worse than the actual pain, gnawing at my insides, hollowing me out.

He climbed onto the bed. The mattress shifted under his weight. His hands roamed my body, exploring the tender flesh he'd just abused. Each touch sent electric shocks of pain and something else—something my mind refused to acknowledge—through me.

"Remember," he said as he positioned himself between my legs, "you earn everything." He reached under my hips and tweaked the butt plug. "And for obeying me and leaving this in like I asked, you've earned an orgasm." He tugged on it again. "As long as you respond to me." He raised an eyebrow at me as he twisted the plug harder.

I flinched, the motion more of a reflex than anything else. A part of me hoped he would take that as the response he was looking for, but I knew better. He wanted me to play along, to pretend, at least, that I was willing.

"Make some noise," he ordered. "Let me know how much you want this."

I bit my lip, hesitating. Then I forced out a moan, soft and unconvincing. He laughed, not fooled, but perhaps amused by my attempt. I heard a click, and the butt plug began to vibrate.

"Oh, fuck!" I exclaimed, the shock forcing my body to arch against the ropes. The sensation was overwhelming, a cruel mix of pleasure and pain that I wasn't prepared for.

My mind scrambled to find that safe place again, but the vibrations made it impossible to detach completely.

"That's better," he said, clearly enjoying my reaction. "See? It's not so hard to do what you're told."

He leaned down and kissed my chest, then bit at my nipple. The pain spiked through me like a needle. The vibrations from the plug sent waves through my core, each building on the last. An unwanted heat grew between my legs, a traitorous response that made me sick with shame. He noticed, of course, and his eyes lit up with perverse delight.

"You're getting wet," he noted with satisfaction, glancing at my increasing arousal. "Maybe this won't take as long as I thought."

He cupped my ass with one hand, pressing against the plug with more force. I let out a strangled cry—half sob, half moan. My hips bucked involuntarily, seeking either relief or more torment—I couldn't tell which.

He plunged a finger inside me—cold and clinical, like a scalpel slicing through my last vestiges of control. He worked it around, testing the resistance. My body twitched and spasmed, each movement a puppet's jerk on invisible strings.

"See how your body responds?" he said, almost marveling. "It knows what it wants, even if you don't."

I didn't want this. I didn't want any of it. But he was right—my body was betraying me in ways my mind couldn't suppress. The heat, the tension, the unbearable tightness coiling in my stomach—it was all rushing toward an inevitable conclusion that I dreaded and craved in equal measure.

He added a second finger and pumped vigorously,

simultaneously rubbing his thumb over my clit. "That's it, doll. I'm going to make this tight pussy weep. You'll be begging for my cock by the time I'm done."

My traitorous body squeezed around his fingers, and the obscene heat of humiliation bloomed across my face. "Fuck," I hissed through clenched teeth, my voice trembling with outrage and unwanted desire.

"There it is," he murmured approvingly, curling his fingers inside me to hit a spot that sent a jolt of sensation up my spine. "That's the response I've been waiting for."

He pumped his fingers harder, and the sounds of my slick flesh melding with the relentless vibration of the plug grew louder. My muscles clenched involuntarily around his fingers, each of his thrusts sending shockwaves through my hypersensitive nerves. I bit down on my lip, desperately trying to stifle the moans clawing their way up my throat.

"You can do better than that," he taunted, smacking the inside of my thigh with his free hand. Pain lanced through me, and I couldn't hold back the raw cry that escaped.

"That's more like it," he said, quickening his pace. "Music to my ears. Give me a good response, and you'll get a good dinner tonight. Keep holding back, and you'll go hungry."

White-hot tension coiled in my core, building with unbearable intensity as his fingers worked me open. My vision blurred at the edges, reality dissolving under the onslaught of conflicting sensations. The vibrations from the butt plug and his relentless fingers created a hurricane of sensation, each gust threatening to tear me apart.

I was on the brink, teetering over an edge I didn't want to fall from. The thought of release filled me equally with dread and relief. How much longer could I endure this? How much longer could I resist?

"Please," I heard myself say, the word slipping out unbidden. "Please…"

He paused, and for a moment, hope flickered in my chest—hope that he would stop, that he'd have some twisted mercy and let me be. But his grin told another story.

"Please, what?" he asked, withdrawing his fingers slowly, agonizingly, leaving me empty and throbbing.

I swallowed hard. "Please…don't stop."

The words tasted like bile in my mouth, but I knew what he wanted to hear. He needed my complicity, my surrender. And perhaps if I gave him that, it would all be over quicker.

His laugh was low and smug, the sound of a man who believed he'd won. He slid his fingers back inside me, torturously slow.

"Beg for it," he said. "Beg me to let you come."

I closed my eyes, retreating to my last refuge—the darkness behind my eyelids, where I could almost pretend I was somewhere else. Somewhere safe.

"Please…" The word was a whisper, an exhalation of breath that cost me more than I could afford to give. "Please let me come."

The plug's vibrations made it hard to focus, hard to think. Each wave of sensation was like a tide, eroding the shoreline of my willpower.

"Say it like you mean it," he demanded, pumping in and out of me a few times before stopping. He flicked his thumb over my swollen, sensitive clit. My body tensed in anticipation, every nerve on high alert. The slowing of his hand was a cruel tease, a promise that he could draw this out indefinitely.

"Please," I said louder, forcing the words through gritted teeth as I opened my eyes. "Please make me come. I need it."

He studied me for a moment, gauging the sincerity in my voice. I willed myself not to flinch under his gaze, not to show the fear and loathing churning inside me.

"That's better," he said finally, resuming his thrusts with more fervor. His thumb rubbed over my clit in firm, deliberate circles. The combined sensations were too much. My back arched against the ropes, muscles seizing with anticipation.

Each flick and thrust sent a surge of electricity through me, short-circuiting my mind and turning my thoughts into a hazy, incoherent mess. The tension in my core wound tighter and tighter, a spring about to snap.

"Come on," he coaxed, his voice a velvet dagger. "Come for me. Show me how much you like it."

I didn't need to show him anything; my body was doing it all on its own. The heat between my legs had become a blazing inferno, the kind that razes entire forests in a single night. Each stroke of his fingers fanned the flames higher, each vibration from the plug an accelerant. I was burning alive, and there was no escaping it.

A sob wrenched from my chest as the first spasms hit. Pleasure crashed over me like a tidal wave, drowning me. My hips bucked and twisted uncontrollably, riding the crest of each new surge. Wetness trickled down my thighs, as my body gave in with obscene squelching sounds. His hand never let up, driving me through the peak and into painful aftershocks.

He clicked off the butt plug, and my body heaved around the stillness like it was letting out a breath it had been holding for an eternity. My hips groaned in relief as the ropes on my legs went lax. But it was only a temporary respite as he passed the ropes attached to my feet behind my neck and pulled taut, pulling my ankles up toward my ears. I was as exposed and vulnerable as I could possibly be.

"Look at that sweet pussy. So hot and wet and ready for me." He positioned himself between my legs and slapped my clit with his erect dick. "Moment of truth," he said roughly as he teased his tip at my entrance. "Let's see if this cunt is worth what I paid for it."

He thrust into me in one brutal, unapologetic punch. A scream tore from my throat as he buried himself to the hilt, painfully stretching and filling me. There was no easing in, no gentle preamble—just an unforgiving invasion that left me gasping.

"Oh, fuck yes," he groaned, his voice thick with satisfaction. "You're so fucking tight. Your greedy pussy is choking on my cock."

His hands gripped my thighs hard enough to bruise as he pulled back and slammed into me again. The force of it rocked my whole body, sending ripples through my flesh. I clenched around him involuntarily, trying to accommodate his relentless thrusting.

"Look at you." He panted, eyes gleaming with a savage light. "Taking my cock like a perfect slut. You're practically swallowing me whole."

I wanted to deny him the satisfaction, but my body betrayed me once more. The sensations were too overwhelming—each brutal thrust sent a mix of pain and unwanted pleasure radiating through my core. Heat and wetness spread between my legs, making every move slick and vulgar.

He leaned forward, changing the angle, driving even deeper into me. His hips pistoned back and forth in an unforgiving rhythm. "Fuck, I can see your pussy stretching to take me," he grunted, thrusting harder. "Every time I slam into you, it's like this tight little cunt is trying to suck me in."

His words were a dark, filthy litany that heightened every sensation. The ropes dug into my flesh, keeping me spread open and utterly at his mercy. My body rocked with each brutal thrust, making obscene noises as his slick cock drove deeper into me.

"You're dripping all over me," he taunted, slamming into me with even more force. "You're soaking my balls, you dirty little whore."

I bit down on my lip to keep from crying out, but it was useless. Each relentless plunge tore moans and gasps from my throat, despite my best efforts to stay silent.

He grinned down at me, eyes glittering with cruel indulgence as he watched my struggle. "That's right," he said roughly. "I wanna hear you scream for it."

Just when I thought I couldn't take another second of his punishing thrusts, he pulled out as quickly as he had punched in. The sudden emptiness was a shock to my system, leaving me gasping and disoriented.

"Don't think I'm done," he growled, stroking his slick cock as he looked down at me with predatory eyes. "I haven't forgotten about that ass that you've so kindly been prepping for me."

A cold dread settled over me. He moved swiftly,

untying the ropes that held my legs and wrists. My limbs were numb and useless, like wet rags, and I couldn't have resisted even if I'd tried. He hauled me up and dragged me to a contraption that looked like a giant high-heeled shoe, its leather surface a deep burgundy that shone under the light.

I stumbled as he pushed me forward, and I collapsed onto the apparatus. It dug into my abdomen, forcing the air from my lungs in a wheezy gasp. He grabbed my wrists and yanked them down to metal rings on the "toe" of the shoe, snapping cuffs around them. My hands dangled uselessly below me, fingers brushing the floor. My head was flush and spinning from the inverted position.

He moved behind me and spread my legs, fastening leather cuffs around my ankles and securing them to rings at the base of the apparatus. My ass was up in the air, completely exposed.

He stepped back, admiring his handiwork, before pulling out his phone. I heard the sound of the camera shutter as he moved around, snapping photo after photo of me bound and vulnerable. "Perfect," he said as he set aside his phone and moved behind me. He gripped and spread my ass cheeks apart, baring me entirely to his gaze. I shivered involuntarily, and he chuckled at my reaction.

His fingers traced a line down my spine, sending a shiver through my body. "Look at you," he marveled, his voice dripping with cruel satisfaction. "All trussed up like a prize pig, ready for slaughter." His hand gripped the end of the butt plug, twisting it viciously. A strangled cry escaped my lips as he wiggled the plug inside me, each movement stretching and tormenting my already sensitive hole.

"That's what you want, isn't it? You want me to absolutely slaughter this little asshole," he taunted, his breath hot against my skin. "I can feel your ass choking on this plug. Desperate little slut." He pulled it out slowly, deliberately, ensuring I felt every inch of its departure. My body trembled and tensed, fighting to adjust to the sudden emptiness left behind.

"Goddamn," he muttered. "Look at you, gaping like a fucking whore." I heard the camera shutter sound again as he snapped another picture. He crouched down beside me, shoving his phone in front of my face. "Look at this," he ordered.

The screen displayed a close-up photo of my gaping asshole, slick and open. It looked obscene—stretched wide from the plug and glistening with wetness.

"See that?" he sneered, zooming in until every raw detail was magnified. "Your asshole's practically begging for my cock."

His words were daggers stabbing into my already decimated dignity. My cheeks burned with shame and anticipation.

He continued to taunt me, his voice dripping with cruel intent. "You think you're stretched now? Just wait until I'm done with you. That ass will be stretched wider than the fucking Grand Canyon." He chuckled as he stood and circled behind me again. A firm finger tested the stretched rim of my ass. "I can't wait to see the before and after photos."

A moment later, a cold, slick substance was squirted directly onto my exposed asshole. There was no stopping this now.

"As much as I'd love to tear into your ass dry, I'm

feeling generous today," he said mockingly. "Your reward for being such a good little slut."

He drizzled the lube liberally, letting it seep into every crevice before rubbing it in. His fingers worked it around and inside me, preparing me for what was to come. I shivered at the sensation, my body betraying me once again with a mixture of dread and reluctant anticipation.

"Don't get used to this," he warned, his voice dark and filled with promise. "Piss me off, and I'll fuck you raw."

Without further preamble, he positioned himself behind me, his cock pressing against my freshly lubed asshole. He pushed in slowly at first, savoring the resistance as my tight ring tried to deny him entry.

"Fuck," he hissed through gritted teeth. "Even with prep, you're so fucking tight."

The intrusion burned, stretching me wider than I thought possible. Inch by agonizing inch, he forced his way inside, prying me open, splitting me apart. Finally, after what felt like an eternity, he was fully seated, his balls pressing against me, heavy and wet. He paused for a moment, letting out a satisfied groan.

"Mmm," he hummed in satisfaction, his hands gripping my hips. "All the way in. You feel that? Feel how deep I am inside you?"

I couldn't muster a response. My breath came in ragged gasps, each exhale punctuated by a soft whimper as my body struggled to adjust to the intrusion.

"God, you feel good. Part of me wants to just stay like this with your tight ass gripping on to my cock for dear life…"

Then, without warning, he let the beast loose.

He pulled back just enough to generate momentum

before slamming into me with enough force to knock the breath from my lungs. The pain was immediate and searing, radiating through my entire body, tearing a ragged cry from my lips. It felt like he was ripping me apart from the inside out.

"Take it," he growled, his voice thick with lust and cruelty. "Take it all, you filthy fucking whore."

His hips snapped forward with brutal precision, driving his cock deeper into me with each punishing thrust. The room echoed with the vile slap of our flesh meeting, punctuated by his grunts of exertion and my strangled cries.

"You're so fucking tight… Fuck, baby, you feel amazing around my cock," he growled in pleasure. "Especially when you're choking on it." He slapped my ass cheek hard, making me jump and tighten up even more around him. A sadistic chuckle escaped his lips as he slapped me again, this time on the other cheek. "Fuck, you're clenching me like a vise," he groaned. "I bet you love this, don't you? Love being fucked like the worthless whore you are."

"I thought you said I was expensive." The words were out of my mouth before I could think. I squeezed my eyes shut, praying he hadn't heard me. I was wrong.

He froze. "What did you say?"

I was silent and still and tense.

He slapped my ass again. "Bitch, what did you fucking say?"

I swallowed hard, knowing that not speaking would only make things worse. "You said…you said I was expensive," I repeated, my voice small and fragile.

For a moment, there was silence, thick and suffocating. Then he laughed—a harsh, mirthless bark that sent a chill down my spine. "Oh, so the cunt has a sense of humor now?"

He yanked my hair, pulling my head back and straining my neck. The blood rushed to my face even more intensely from the inverted position. "Let me make something clear," he snarled into my ear. "Just because I paid a small fortune for you doesn't mean you're *worth* a fucking cent."

He released my hair and grabbed my hips with both hands, his fingers digging in like talons. With a vicious thrust, he drove himself deep inside me again, setting a brutal pace that left no room for my body to acclimate. The pain was blinding, each stroke like the cut of a serrated knife.

"You're mine now," he spat, his breath coming in ragged bursts. "I fucking own you. That means you've got to earn your worth. Right now, you're nothing but a living fuck toy. A set of holes for me to use."

Anger fueled his every motion. He pounded into me with a violence that bordered on inhuman, each thrust a hammer blow to my insides. My body jolted against the restraints, muscles straining and tearing under the assault. The pain was all-consuming, leaving no room for thought or feeling beyond the immediate agony of his cock ravaging me.

"Is this what you wanted?" he barked, his breath hot and ragged. "Wanted me to fuck you harder? To treat you like the cheap slut you are?"

I couldn't respond. My mouth opened and closed soundlessly, my lungs unable to draw enough air to form even a single word. My vision blurred, teetering on the edge of unconsciousness.

He didn't care. He was lost in his primal need, using

my body with total disregard for my well-being. Or my humanity.

His pace grew erratic, more desperate. He was close. "Fuck," he groaned, his hips losing their brutal rhythm. "Gonna fill this tight little ass…"

With a final, devastating thrust, he buried himself as deep as he could. The hot rush of his cum hit my insides as he unloaded, each spurt accompanied by a shudder and a guttural moan. He held me there, impaled on his cock, letting every drop seep into me.

Just when I thought he was done, he pulled out quickly, the sudden emptiness making me gasp. The last few strands of cum shot out, splattering against my skin like hot wax. He let out a contented sigh.

"Stay just like that," he commanded.

Like I had a choice.

I heard the camera click again as he took his "after" photo. "Perfect," he muttered, clearly pleased with his work.

My body was a wreck—every muscle trembling, every nerve frayed. I stayed perfectly still, too afraid and dazed to move or speak.

He walked over to a small cooler in the corner and pulled out a bottle of water. The plastic crinkled as he unscrewed the cap, took a swig, and then wiped his mouth with the back of his hand. He walked over to me, my body still quivering from the ordeal, and held the bottle near my face. The cool condensation dripped onto my skin.

"Thirsty?" he asked, almost casually.

I nodded weakly, too exhausted to even lift my head. He inserted a straw and brought it to my lips. I sucked at it ravenously, the cold water rushing into my parched mouth and down my throat with a relief so intense it was almost painful.

He let me drink for a few moments before pulling it away. "What do you say for the water?" he asked, his tone expectant.

"Thank you," I managed, my voice hoarse but sincere. I knew better than to show defiance now.

He crouched beside me and smiled—a predatory, satisfied curve of his lips. "And what do you say for my cock?"

A wave of nausea rushed through me, bile rising in my throat. I swallowed hard, knowing that hesitation would only prolong this. "Thank you," I said, forcing the words out like broken glass. "Thank you for your cock."

"Good girl," he said, almost fondly. He brought the straw back to my lips. "You can have some more."

I drank slowly this time, until my hands and jaw stopped shaking. The water's coolness seeped into my core, momentarily dulling the acute pain that radiated from every part of my body.

He pulled the straw away, stood, and walked to a small table to retrieve his phone. "I think you'll want to see this," he said, swiping at the screen. He crouched down beside me again and held the phone in front of my face.

On the screen was a high-resolution photo of my ass, gaping and red and raw from his abuse, a trail of his cum leaking out and mixing with the lube that was smeared across my skin. Bruises were already forming where his hands had gripped me too tightly.

I stared at the image, a mixture of disgust and numbness washing over me. He held the phone there longer than necessary, savoring my reaction. When he was satisfied, he stood, put on a garish-looking dressing gown, and pocketed the device.

"You did well," he said, tying the sash at his waist. "But I can't let that little mouthy moment earlier go unpunished."

My heart sank. I knew speaking out would cost me, but hearing him confirm it hollowed my stomach.

"So here's the deal," he continued. "You can have food or sleep, but not both."

The choice was torture in itself. My body screamed for nourishment, but the thought of enduring another session with him on an empty tank of rest was unbearable.

"Sleep," I whispered, barely audible.

He shrugged. "If that's what you want." He walked to the door and paused, turning back to look at me. "We'll pick this up tomorrow. Maybe then you'll be worth something."

With that, he flicked off the light. The room plunged into darkness, and the door creaked open.

"Good night," he sang in a sickly sweet, taunting voice.

"Wait!" I cried.

"Yes?" He drew out the word longer than necessary.

"Are you going to unchain me?" I asked, my voice trembling with my last ounce of hope.

He was silent for a moment, and I held my breath, awaiting his reply. "No," he said finally. "You can stay just like that and think about being more obedient. If you want to sleep in a bed, earn it."

The door slammed shut, and I heard the click of the lock turning. He was gone.

I was alone.

I lay there in the darkness, my body a constellation of

pain from where he had struck and gripped and thrust. The excess lube and his cum were drying and crusting on my skin. Each breath sent a new wave of agony through my ribs and lungs.

The dam inside me finally broke. Sobs racked my body, each one a tidal wave of sorrow and fear that crashed against my already fragile frame. I cried for the pain, for the hopelessness of my situation, for the life I had lost. Hot tears plopped onto the leather and pooled around my face. There was no one to hear me, no one to care.

Time stretched and distorted in the pitch black of the room. Minutes felt like hours, hours like days. My mind drifted in and out of a hazy, painful semi-consciousness— the twilight state where dreams and reality blur together, but none of it offers any true escape.

The sobs eventually subsided as the last of my energy drained away, and at some point, sleep mercifully claimed me.

groom

. . .

"WAKEY, WAKEY."

Harsh light flooded the room, and I squinted against it, my eyes burning from the sudden brightness. My body protested as I tried to move, every muscle raw and unyielding.

A sharp gasp escaped my lips as reality rushed back. I was still bent over the smooth leather furniture, my wrists and ankles locked in place, my body exposed like a piece of meat in a butcher's window.

He stood above me, fully dressed in a tailored suit that gave him an air of cold professionalism, as if he were about to conduct a business meeting rather than…

"Nice to see you're still in one piece." His tone was almost cheerful. Straightening his tie, he looked down at me with an appraising eye, running a hand up the back of my thigh before resting it on my ass. "Sleep well, my dear?"

I didn't respond. My mind was moving sluggishly, still

gripped by the fog of exhaustion. Every part of me ached —a deep, gnawing throb that sapped my will to even be afraid.

My stomach growled loudly, the sound almost feral in the quiet room.

He smirked and removed his hand from my ass. "You're going to need your strength. Be a good girl, and you'll get breakfast."

He reached into his pocket, pulled out a key, then bent down and unlocked my wrists and ankles. The metal clinked softly as it fell away, and I collapsed to the floor in a heap, my body too weak to support itself.

"Thank me," he commanded, standing over me with the key still in his hand.

"Thank you," I said, my voice a cracked whisper. I struggled to sit up, every movement sending sharp stabs of pain through my muscles.

"For what?" he asked, his tone mocking.

I closed my eyes and took a slow, painful breath. "Thank you for unchaining me."

"Good girl." Finally, something I did pleased him. "Now remember the rules—naked, clean, and shaven at all times."

I nodded slowly, each movement of my head feeling like it might topple me.

He looked me up and down with disdain. "You're filthy. Still covered in my cum. Did you forget my rules already?"

I opened my mouth to protest, to say that it wasn't my fault, that he had left me chained up with no way to clean myself. But I closed it just as quickly, biting down on my lower lip. Excuses would only make things worse. This was part of his game, and I needed to play this right if I was going to survive.

He studied me for a moment, perhaps waiting for the outburst I'd wisely swallowed. "I'll overlook it this once," he said finally. "Since you're new."

A flicker of relief sparked within me, but I tamped it down just as quickly. This was no mercy.

"Come," he said, turning on his heel and walking toward a door on the far side of the room. I hesitated for a moment, then forced myself to stand. My legs wobbled beneath me, unsteady and weak from their prolonged confinement.

The door led to an ensuite bathroom, marble surfaces gleaming under recessed lighting. It was opulent, like something out of a high-end hotel—a jarring contrast to the stark brutality of the other room. I caught a glimpse of myself in the mirror—just long enough to feel sick. I dropped my gaze to the floor, unable to face the wreck staring back at me.

He stood by the open walk-in shower, turned on the water, and tested the temperature with his hand. Steam began to billow around him, creating a humid haze that softened the sharp lines of the marble.

"Get in," he commanded, stepping back and crossing his arms over his chest. I hesitated at the threshold, the thought of hot water on my broken skin both enticing and terrifying.

Slowly, I hobbled to the shower and stepped inside. There was no door. The tiles were slick and warm under my feet, and the water cascaded over me like molten glass, stinging every cut and bruise. I bit down hard on my lip to keep from crying out.

He pulled out a chair from the corner of the bathroom and sat down, legs spread casually, hands resting on his knees, eyes watching my every move. "Don't dawdle," he said. "You have ten minutes to get yourself clean and shaven."

I found a bar of soap in a recessed niche and slathered it between my hands. The suds were slippery and uncooperative as I tried to scrub my body clean. Each pass over my skin was a new lesson in pain, but the thought of being free of his residue spurred me on.

Watching in silence, his eyes never left me. They were predatory, studying every movement with a cold intensity. I tried to block him out, to pretend I was alone and safe, but his gaze tracked my every thought and fear, stripping away any illusion of privacy or dignity.

I washed and rinsed my hair and then set about the task that seemed to interest him the most. My fingers were pruned and sore as I reached for the razor, my hands unsteady with fatigue. I took a deep breath and began to shave, each stroke a calculated risk. The hot water had softened my skin to the point where even the lightest pressure could nick me, and any cut would be a new source of agony.

He leaned back in his chair, stretching, his demeanor one of smug satisfaction. "Careful now," he said. "Don't damage my property."

I bit down on my cheek and focused on the task, trying to make each movement precise despite my shaking hands. The steam had coated the mirror in a foggy film, softening the edges of my reflection. I could look now, but only because I couldn't really see myself. Just the faint outline of a body—ghostly, frail, like a wisp of smoke ready to vanish.

I gently set the razor on the shelf next to the shampoo and rinsed any remaining residue. Water swirled with white streaks of soap and escaped down the drain.

"Enough," he barked. "Get out."

I turned off the water and stepped onto the mat. The cooler air of the bathroom kissed my skin, causing goosebumps to rise.

"Dry off."

He tossed me a towel, and I caught it with clumsy hands.

"Dry off," he repeated, his eyes drilling into me as I slowly patted the towel over my skin. Each touch was a new revelation of pain, and I moved with the caution of someone handling a live grenade. The warmth from the shower began to leach away.

"Now kneel," he commanded.

My heart sank as I let the towel fall to the floor next to me and lowered myself onto my knees. The marble was hard and unyielding, sending sharp jolts up my tender legs. I knelt before him like a penitent sinner awaiting absolution, my body caving in on itself with exhaustion and fear.

He leaned forward, his hands resting on his knees, and regarded me with clinical detachment. "Let's see how you did," he said, reaching out to run a hand over my shaved pussy. The touch was light but invasive, like a doctor's examination. I tensed, every muscle in my body coiling like a spring.

"Good job," he said, almost surprised. "You're smooth." Withdrawing his hand, he sat back in his chair, crossing one leg over the other. "Remember, you're to always be clean and ready for me. Don't forget again."

I nodded, too afraid and too tired to say anything.

He stood. "I'm going to step out. You have five minutes to relieve yourself, brush your teeth, and generally make yourself presentable. Do that, and you'll earn your breakfast."

comply

. . .

MY "BREAKFAST" consisted of a single mealy apple, a chalky chocolate protein shake, and a bottle of water. But I downed it like a gourmet meal. Once I'd finished the last sip of the shake, I set the empty bottle down with a trembling hand. My body was still in survival mode, and the rush of even that paltry nutrition made me dizzy. I wiped my mouth with the back of my hand and looked up at him. He was seated in a leather armchair, legs crossed, typing on his phone.

Slowly, I rose from where I had been sitting on the floor and moved to kneel at his feet. He continued to ignore me. My heart pounded in my chest. I knew what he wanted.

"Thank you for the breakfast," I said softly, my voice just strong enough to carry.

He clicked off his phone and set it on a side table next to a long black velvet box. "You're welcome," he said, his tone almost warm. Almost. "It's nice to see you're learning some manners."

A flicker of hope sparked within me. Perhaps he would

let me truly rest now, let me recover enough to handle whatever came next. But that hope was quickly obliterated.

"We have a visitor, so I want you on your best behavior."

I dropped my head.

"And I have a gift for you."

I looked back up at him as he retrieved the box off the side table and opened it. Inside was a leather collar studded with diamonds, fastened with a ruby-crusted clasp.

He fastened the collar around my neck, his fingers brushing against my skin with chilling intimacy. The leather was stiff and unyielding. The clasp locked with an unforgiving click.

His voice was low and measured. "This will serve as a reminder that you belong to me." Two fingers tugged roughly at the leather, ensuring the collar was securely fastened.

He sat back in his chair and retrieved his phone from the side table. With a few swipes and taps, he opened an app, then turned the screen toward me. It displayed a blinking dot on a map, along with various settings and controls. "The collar has an embedded tracking device," he said. "So don't bother trying to escape."

I stared at the screen, my mind racing through the implications. Even if I could get away from him physically, there would be no hiding. No sanctuary where he couldn't find me.

"And if you do get any bright ideas about escaping or disobeying me..." He trailed off, looking down at his phone. His finger hovered over the screen for a moment, then pressed down.

A searing jolt shot through the collar and into my neck,

spreading like wildfire through my nervous system. My body convulsed, muscles seizing and spasming beyond my control. A strangled cry ripped from my throat as I collapsed to the floor, every nerve ending alight with unbearable pain.

He leaned forward, his eyes glittering with a dangerous satisfaction. "I hope that will motivate you to be an obedient slave," he said, each word dripping with condescension. "And enthusiastic in your duties."

I lay on the floor, gasping for breath, my body a wreckage of pain and fear.

"Follow me to my office." He rose from his chair, phone in hand, then paused at the doorway and looked back at me. "Now."

I scrambled up on shaking arms and stumbled after him.

The house was a monument to excess, each room more opulent and gaudier than the last. Gold leaf adorned the walls, and crystal chandeliers hung from vaulted ceilings. Expensive works of art were strewn about with a careless arrogance, as if their presence alone could confer taste.

We reached his office at the end of a long hallway. It was a cavernous room lined with mahogany bookshelves and dominated by an enormous desk. Seated in a guest chair in front of the desk was an older man, perhaps in his sixties, with a poorly fitted toupee that looked like it might scurry off his head at any moment. He wore khaki slacks, a white collared shirt, and a powder blue sweater vest. When he saw us enter, a greasy smile spread across his face.

"Doctor," my captor said, walking around to sit behind the desk. "Thank you for coming on such short notice."

Fear gripped my heart as I processed his words. A doctor. My eyes flicked to the older man, and a wave of ick and dread washed over me. There was a hunger in his eyes that made my skin crawl. If I thought my captor was a villain, the doctor exuded something far worse—pure, unfiltered evil.

"It's always a pleasure," the doctor said, his gaze roaming over me. His voice was oily. "I see she's coming along nicely."

My master—could I even call him that? The word felt too gentle for what he was—steepled his fingers and regarded me with the same cold calculation as before. "She is, but I want to make sure she's in peak condition. Your expert opinion is invaluable."

I stood frozen.

The doctor stood and stalked toward me, leather satchel in hand. He paused and pointed behind me to a gynecologic chair in the corner of the office. "Up you go," he said, his voice dripping with anticipation.

Who has a gyno chair in a home office?

I looked to my master, silently pleading. He met my gaze and gave a slow, deliberate nod. When I didn't move quickly enough, he pulled out his phone and let his finger hover over the screen.

Terror shot through me. The memory of the collar's electric bite was too fresh, too vivid. I rushed to the chair and climbed up with trembling hands, lying back against the cold vinyl. Leg restraints and stirrups projected from the examination table like sinister ornaments.

The doctor looked at the stirrups and back at me. "I believe you know what to do with your legs."

I hesitated briefly, my mind a whirl of fear and revulsion. Then, with slow, reluctant movements, I lifted my legs and placed my feet in the stirrups. The position made me feel horribly exposed, but there was no point in resisting.

My master chuckled. "Better get used to it. I like a nice view when I work. And a good distraction…"

The doctor fastened leather straps around my ankles, knees, wrists, and waist, securing me firmly to the table. He patted the inside of my thigh. "We wouldn't want you to flinch and hurt yourself," he said, his tone mocking.

The doctor set his satchel on a nearby table and began rummaging through it. "Should I give her something to make her more docile?" he asked without looking up.

I stared at the ceiling and started counting the crystals dangling from the ornate black and gold chandelier.

"No," my master replied. "I don't like my girls strung out the way you do. It's like fucking a ragdoll."

The doctor let out a small, humorless chuckle. "To each his own," he said, snapping on examination gloves with deliberate slowness. The sound echoed in the cavernous office like the crack of a whip.

I squeezed my eyes shut, every muscle in my body tensed for the inevitable violation. The doctor's gloved hands made contact with my most vulnerable place, and I flinched despite myself.

"I can see you've already taken her for a nice ride," the doctor said, his voice thick with something like admiration. He spread me open with clinical detachment, but his words betrayed a lecherous fascination.

I bit down on my lip so hard I tasted blood. The pain was a welcome distraction from the indignity of his touch.

"She's supposed to have an IUD," my master said. "I want to make sure it's still in place."

The doctor muttered something under his breath, then inserted two fingers, probing deeper. A sharp pain lanced through me, and I sucked in a breath through clenched teeth. He wiggled his fingers, stretching me beyond comfort and into pain.

"Everything looks in order," the doctor said, not withdrawing his hand. "The device is in place. So, what are your intentions? Do you plan to breed her?"

My eyes flew open. *Breed me*? The thought was too horrifying to contemplate.

"Hell no," my master said, almost laughing. "I'm not looking for that kind of commitment. All I want her for is fucking."

"What a pity." The doctor clicked his tongue and licked his lips. "She's a fine specimen." His hand lingered longer than necessary before he finally withdrew it, and my body sagged with a mixture of relief and ongoing dread. "If you like, I can perform a more permanent procedure. It would save you trouble in the long run."

My master shook his head. "The IUD will do for now. I just got her. I don't want her out of commission from a surgery just yet."

A tense silence filled the room. I dared not move or speak, my mind racing through the possibilities of what these men could still do to me.

My master rose from his chair and walked around the desk, stopping in front of me. He looked down, not at me but at the obscene position of my legs. "Doctor," he said slowly, "what do you recommend to prepare her for tonight?"

A cruel grin spread across the doctor's face. He reached into his satchel and pulled out a small packet. "This will do the trick," the doctor said. "Dissolve one square on her tongue and rub the ointment on her clit. She'll be so eager and so desperate for release, she'll fuck the doorknobs if she has to." His grin widened.

A low chuckle rumbled from my master, and he took the packet from the doctor's hand, examining it with interest before tucking it into his pocket. "Sounds perfect. You're coming tonight, right?"

"Of course," the doctor said, peeling off his gloves with a soft pop. "I'll bring my Kitten along."

My master nodded, a slow smile creeping across his face. "She'll be a good example for this one," he said, indicating me with a tilt of his head.

I shuddered in the chair, the restraints biting into my skin. Tonight. They were planning something for tonight, and it involved more than just these two monsters.

My master started toward the door, then paused and looked back at me. "Doctor, I'll leave you to collect your fee."

With that, he exited the office, closing the door softly behind him.

The doctor's gaze lingered on the closed door for a moment before shifting back to me. The greasy smile from earlier returned, more depraved than ever, his voice a low, hungry growl as he said, "I would tell you to spread"—he unbuckled his belt and undid his fly—"but you're already in the perfect position."

He moved with the practiced ease of a man who had done this many times before, pushing his pants down to his knees and stroking himself to readiness. Terror and revulsion surged through me as I realized what he intended. My mind screamed, but my voice was trapped deep in my throat. I knew that begging would do no good. It would probably only excite him more.

The doctor stepped closer, his breath hot on my skin as he loomed over me. "You might even enjoy it," he said, more to himself than to me.

He positioned himself between my legs, teasing me, but then paused as if struck by a thought. I shut my eyes tight, bracing for the worst.

"Your master should have let you take the sedative," he mused, almost regretfully. "It would have been kinder."

For a brief, foolish second, I hoped he might show some mercy and spare me.

"Oh well."

The first thrust was brutal. I gasped in pain, my body jerking against the restraints. He gripped my hips and pulled me hard against him, setting a violent rhythm that sent waves of agony through my core. Each stroke felt like a stab wound. The pain was unbearable. I was still sore and raw from the previous night, and the doctor's violent penetration tore at me like broken glass.

He fucked me like a beast, as if consuming me piece by piece. The room grew hotter, more stifling, and his sweat dripped onto my skin. His hands roamed my body, squeezing my breasts, then digging into my thighs with a feral need.

Gripping my hips so tightly I knew there would be marks, he pulled me against him with a force that sent shockwaves through my entire body. His breathing grew heavier, more labored—each exhale a hot, fetid blast against my skin. I tried to dissociate, to imagine myself somewhere—anywhere—else, but the sheer physicality of his assault kept yanking me back to the present.

The doctor let out a series of low, animalistic grunts. "So tight," he muttered, almost in disbelief. "If you were mine, I'd fuck you day in and day out."

A sob caught in my throat. The bastard was enjoying this even more than my master had. As monstrous as my captor was, he at least took some perverse pride in my reactions. The doctor cared only for his own gratification.

He shifted his angle and drove deeper. A scream burst from my lips, echoing off the office walls. The sound seemed to excite him as he quickened his pace, each thrust more punishing than the last. My screams dissolved into whimpers, then into a numb silence as my body went limp with resignation. The pain had reached a plateau, a constant, searing burn that I could no longer distinguish from the rest of me.

His grunts grew louder, more urgent, and his movements became erratic. He was close. A grotesque hope flared within me. The sooner he finished, the sooner this would be over.

With a final, violent shove, he buried himself to the hilt and let out a long, disgusting groan. His body convulsed against mine as he emptied himself inside me, and I felt a rush of nauseous relief wash over me. It was done.

He lingered, catching his breath, then slowly pulled out. A mixture of fluids trickled down my buttocks, and I fought the urge to retch.

I lay there, shattered and motionless, as he casually pulled his pants back up.

He looked down at me with a self-satisfied smirk, wiping the sweat from his forehead with the back of his hand. "You were better than I expected," he said, fastening his belt. "I'll enjoy fucking you again tonight."

I didn't respond.

I couldn't.

perform

. . .

"OPEN YOUR MOUTH," my master commanded. He held a small square on the tip of his index finger.

I opened my mouth as instructed, and he placed the square on my tongue. It dissolved quickly, leaving a bitter taste that made me wince. He knelt between my legs. His touch was surprisingly gentle as he applied ointment, rubbing it in slow circles on my clit. A spark of unwanted pleasure shot through me.

He walked me to the adjoining room, where soft lighting cast long shadows on plush furniture. A large X-frame stood ominously in the center, its leather cuffs dangling like beckoning hands. My master guided me to it, and I didn't resist—there was no point. He strapped my wrists and ankles in place and tested each bond to ensure it was tight.

The drug was already starting to take hold, leaving my head light and my body uncomfortably aware of every touch, every brush of fabric. A warmth spread from my core, tingling across my skin, making every nerve ending hyperaware. My clit throbbed with an unbearable heat, as if it would explode. I tugged at the restraints, my body already craving a touch—any touch—to quench the burning need.

My master stepped back, admiring his work. "You are the entertainment tonight," he said, his voice smooth and measured.

I could barely focus on his words. The heat in my clit was spreading, mingling with the drug-induced euphoria, creating a storm of sensations that threatened to consume me. I bit down on my lip, trying to stifle the moan that was building in my chest.

"You will please my guests in whatever way they desire. If you perform well, I'll allow you to sleep in a bed tonight."

A bed. The promise of something so simple and so distant from the horrors of the last few days made my heart ache with longing. Could I survive whatever they had planned? Would a bed even bring me any comfort if I did?

The drug surged through my veins, making me feral and jittery, like an animal in heat. I breathed in shallow gasps.

He left me there, bound and exposed, and walked to the door. As he opened it, excited chatter spilled in from the hallway. My heart pounded in my ears.

"Come in," my master said, stepping aside to let them in.

They entered in a loose cluster—all men wearing expensive suits and sporting the kind of casual arrogance that comes from old money. They carried drinks, and the scents of liquor and cologne mingled in the air. The soft murmur of their voices was interrupted by occasional bursts of laughter.

One of the men, tall with graying temples, approached the X-frame first. He looked me up and down, his gaze cold and detached as if appraising a piece of art. He ran a finger along my thigh, then turned to my master. "She's exquisite. Well done!"

Another man joined the first, shorter and stockier but with the same air of entitlement. He whistled low and slow, clapping my master on the shoulder. "How much did she set you back?"

"More than I wanted to spend," my master replied, "but she's worth every penny." He raised his glass. "Enough talk. Tonight is about enjoyment. Please, make yourselves at home and savor the entertainment."

The men needed no further encouragement. The tall one with graying temples leaned in first, his lips brushing my ear as he whispered, "Let's see how you scream." He pinched my nipple hard, twisting it between his fingers. A jolt of pain shot through me, but the drug twisted it into perverse pleasure, and I let out a high, breathy moan.

Hands were everywhere. One man stroked my inner thigh, teasingly close to my burning center but never quite touching it. Another tugged at my hair, pulling my head back to expose my neck, which he then grazed with his teeth. My body was a live wire, every touch sending sparks flying through me. I couldn't tell whose hands were where —they blended in a haze of sensation.

Someone slipped a hand between my legs, fingers parting me. I thrust my hips forward, desperate for more, but the fingers withdrew just as quickly as they had come. I whimpered in frustration.

"She's already wet," he said with a grin. "You really know how to prepare them."

My master smiled, swirling the liquid in his glass.

The men leered at me, their hands becoming more aggressive as they squeezed and pinched and groped. The tall one with graying temples slid his fingers between my legs again, this time plunging them inside me without warning. I gasped, the sensation unbearable and electrifying all at once. He curled his fingers, hitting that spot inside me that sent a jolt of pleasure through my core.

"Look at her," he said, his voice dripping with condescension as he pumped his fingers in and out. "She's practically begging for it."

I tried to stifle my moans, but each thrust of his fingers made it harder to contain the sounds bubbling up my throat. The drug pulsed through me, amplifying every touch until I was a writhing mess.

Another man—the shorter, stockier one—moved in front of me and tugged roughly at my nipples. He didn't bother with teasing, just latched his mouth onto one breast while twisting the other nipple hard between his thumb and forefinger. The dual sensation of pain and pleasure made me arch my back involuntarily, pressing my chest further into his face. He bit down on my nipple, eliciting a strangled cry from me.

The door opened again, and the doctor from earlier entered. Even with the drug coursing through my system, my blood ran cold. He held a leash in one hand, and a small, slight woman with dark hair tied into pigtails crawled in after him. She wore nothing but a collar attached to the leash and a pair of cat ears. The men turned their attention to the newcomers, smiles spreading across their faces.

"Doctor," my master said, raising his glass in greeting. "We were beginning to wonder if you'd make it."

The doctor shrugged, unperturbed. "Traffic," he said simply, then glanced down at the woman on the leash. "Sit." She obediently sat back on her haunches, her eyes wide and vacant.

"We're glad you're here," said the tall man with graying temples. "Nice of you to bring some extra entertainment."

"Of course," the doctor said, his eyes glinting behind his glasses. He looked down at the woman on the leash and gave a sharp, cruel tug. "Kitten, why don't you show them how it's done?"

A murmur of approval rippled through the men as Kitten crawled on all fours toward me. My heart pounded in my chest, each beat echoing in my ears. The drug had me teetering on the edge, every touch magnified to an almost painful intensity. I knew what was coming, and a part of me—some small, drug-addled corner of my mind —welcomed it.

Kitten rose to her knees in front of me. She looked up briefly, and I saw her eyes were blown wide, pupils dilated to black orbs. High out of her mind.

"Lap her up like milk," the doctor commanded.

Without hesitation, she pressed her face between my legs and began to lick. Her tongue was soft and wet and warm, moving in slow, deliberate strokes. A lightning bolt of pleasure shot through me, and I pressed my lips together to keep from crying out. She flicked her tongue at my clit, sending spasms through my entire body, and I tugged at the restraints, my hips bucking toward her mouth uncontrollably.

The men stepped back and formed a loose circle, like spectators at a sporting event. Their eyes gleamed with anticipation as they sipped their drinks, commenting to each other in low tones.

"Hundred bucks says she screams within a minute."

"You're on," said another, clinking his glass in agreement.

Kitten's tongue worked with an expert's precision, moving in circles and flicks that sent waves of ecstasy crashing over me. The drug had my body primed and ready, every nerve ending crackling under my skin. Heat built in my core, rising faster than I wanted it to. I tried to hold back, knowing that once I came, the true torture would begin. But it was no use. The pleasure was too intense, too immediate.

Kitten's hands came up to my thighs, holding me steady as she buried her face deeper. Her tongue lashed at my clit with a ferocity that bordered on violent. I was right there, teetering on the brink.

"Oh fuck." The words burst unbidden from my lips. My hips ground against Kitten's face, seeking more of her relentless tongue. Sparks danced behind my closed eyes, my breathing ragged and desperate.

"She's gonna blow!" said one of the men, his voice tinged with glee.

"Come on, girl, make her squirt!"

Kitten redoubled her efforts, sucking my clit into her mouth and lashing it with her tongue. The sensation was more than I could bear. My body exploded, every muscle tensing and releasing in a violent wave. I screamed, the sound piercing and raw, bouncing off the walls of the room. My body shook uncontrollably, shuddering with the force of the orgasm as it ripped through me. Kitten didn't stop. She continued to lick and suck, prolonging my climax until it became too much.

"Not even a minute," said the tall man with graying temples, checking his watch with a satisfied smirk. The short, stocky man grumbled and handed over a crisp hundred-dollar bill.

Kitten pulled away, her face glistening, and crawled back to the doctor. I hung limply in the restraints, my body spent but my mind still whirring from the drug. The men talked and laughed among themselves, their voices a distant hum in my ears.

My master set down his empty glass and walked over to me. He unbuckled the straps that held my wrists and ankles, and I collapsed into his arms, too weak to stand on my own.

He held me upright and addressed the room. "Who wants her next?"

The tall man stepped forward, already loosening his belt. "I'll take a turn." He grabbed me roughly by the arm, dragged me over to a large round ottoman, and tossed me onto it. I landed on my back, and he splayed my legs wide open.

"Look at that!" He grasped his cock, already hard and leaking, and without any preamble, sank inside me with a gratified groan.

I gasped, the sudden fullness making my eyes water. The drug twisted the pain into pleasure, and despite myself, I moaned.

Another man stepped forward and positioned himself

in front of me. He had a cruel smile on his face as he rubbed his dick against my lips. "Open wide," he commanded, grabbing a fistful of my hair for leverage. I parted my lips obediently, and he shoved his cock into my mouth with a grunt.

"That's it," he said approvingly as I began to suck. "Good girl."

The men around us hooted and jeered, their excitement palpable. Hands roamed over my body, pinching and groping as the two men fucked me from both ends.

The tall man between my legs set a brutal pace, slamming into me with enough force to make the ottoman creak beneath us. His cock pounded my pussy relentlessly, every thrust sending shockwaves of pleasure through my drug-addled brain. The man at my mouth wasn't any gentler. He fucked my face with feverish intensity, gripping my hair so tight it made my scalp burn.

"Fuck yeah, take it all," one of the men cheered as I gagged and choked around the thick cock driving in and out of my mouth. Another man grabbed my bouncing tits, squeezing them hard before latching his mouth onto a nipple and sucking greedily. My back arched off the ottoman, torn between the electric jolts of pain and pleasure.

Two more men approached, their eyes gleaming with lust. "Bet she's even tighter up the ass," one of them remarked, stroking his cock as he watched another man's dick split my pussy wide open.

My master laughed from his spot against the wall, watching the scene play out with an amused smirk. He swirled his drink lazily before taking a sip. "Who wants to find out?"

Through the clamor of voices, jeers, and grunts, the doctor's voice pierced like a blade. "I've already called first dibs on that ass." The sickening snap of a latex glove echoed through the room.

The men parted to make way as the doctor stepped forward. He grabbed me roughly by the arm, pulled me off the ottoman, and dragged me across the room to a large pommel horse. I stumbled along, still dazed from the drug and the relentless fucking I'd just endured.

He bent me over the padded top and secured my wrists and ankles to the legs with leather straps. My body was folded painfully and exposed, ass high in the air.

"Look at how flexible she is," he taunted, giving the back of my thigh a sharp slap that made me yelp. "Like a fucking gymnast." The men laughed and crowded closer to get a better view.

He moved behind me and spread my ass cheeks wide. Cool air hit tender skin. I shivered at the sensation but didn't have time to dwell on it before his gloved fingers circled my rim. He took his time lubing up my ass, making sure every inch was slick and ready. His touch was almost clinical, but there was an edge of sadistic pleasure in his movements.

"You're going to want this," he taunted. He tapped my diamond-studded collar and leaned close enough to whisper in my ear. "Tell me you want this, or I'll have your master shock you until you're unconscious, and I'll take your ass anyway."

My eyes widened, and my body tensed. I didn't need to feel the bite of the shock collar to know he meant it.

"Please," I whimpered, my voice barely a whisper. "Please fuck my ass."

He chuckled darkly and ran a finger down my spine. "What was that? Speak up, slut."

"Please fuck my ass," I pleaded louder, my voice trembling with fear and anticipation.

The doctor circled me like a predator. "That's right, beg for it," he demanded. He stood behind me again, spreading my ass cheeks with both hands.

"Please," I begged, louder this time so everyone could hear. My face burned with humiliation. "Please fuck my ass."

"Louder!" he barked, slapping my ass hard enough to leave a mark.

"Please fuck my ass!" I screamed, tears welling up in my eyes from the sting of his slap and the shame of my words.

"Good girl," he sneered, then dipped down to lick me from clit to asshole, making me shudder violently. The men around us cheered and hooted their approval.

He probed my tight rim slowly at first, teasing one, then two fingers inside me, stretching my ass and making me gasp. My body trembled with each thrust of his fingers.

"Look at that tight little hole," he cooed, his voice dripping with mockery. "Bet you never thought you'd be begging for this, huh?"

Working his fingers in and out of my ass, he twisted and scissored them, opening me up. I writhed against the restraints.

"Fuck yeah, stretch her out," one of the men encouraged, his hand pumping over his cock.

The doctor smirked and redoubled his efforts, shoving his fingers in deep and curling them inside me, the sensation making my back arch and my breath hitch. He spread his fingers wide, stretching me open before pulling out almost entirely and brutally slamming back in.

"Bet you like that, don't you?" he sneered, pumping three fingers in and out of my ass. "Fucking slut."

I couldn't help the whimper that escaped my lips. The feeling of being so full, so stretched, was overwhelming. My body trembled uncontrollably, teetering on the edge of what I could endure. He worked his fingers with ruthless efficiency, each movement calculated to maximize my discomfort—and my forced arousal.

"Fist her!" one of the men shouted, his voice thick with arousal. "Stretch her out good."

The doctor chuckled, withdrawing his fingers slowly. The empty feeling was almost a relief. "I'd like her to still be tight around my cock," he said as he peeled off his glove. "But feel free to fist her when I'm done."

My heart pounded in my chest as I heard the rustle of fabric and saw the doctor's slacks pool at his ankles behind me.

"Here," the doctor said as he handed something to one of the other men. "Make her come while I fuck her ass," he ordered.

A click, followed by the unmistakable high-pitched whine of a vibrator.

Fuck.

The doctor moved into position behind me, the blunt head of his cock pressing against my stretched rim.

He didn't ease in. He drove himself deep into my ass with one brutal thrust.

I screamed.

"Fuck, that's tight!" The doctor grunted as he buried

himself. My body seized up, muscles spasming around the cock stretching my ass beyond its limits.

The man with the vibrator moved between my legs, positioning the toy right against my clit, sending jolts of sensation through my already hypersensitive flesh. The mix of pleasure and pain was overwhelming.

The doctor grabbed my hips for leverage and started fucking me hard and fast, his cock slamming in and out of my ass with a relentless rhythm. "Take it," he snarled, slapping my ass for emphasis. "Take this big cock up your slutty ass."

I could barely breathe, each thrust driving the air from my lungs and making me gasp. The vibrator buzzed against my clit, amplified by the drug still coursing through me and the ointment making me burn. My body was torn between the agony of being stretched so brutally and the desperate need to come.

As the vibrator relentlessly tortured my clit, sending wave after wave of forced pleasure through my trembling body, that awful tightness built inside me. Every nerve was on fire, my muscles clenching and spasming around the thick cock invading my ass.

"Look at her squirm," one of the men taunted as he watched me struggle.

The doctor let out a guttural laugh, his grip on my hips tightening as he pounded into me even harder. "I love how tight they get when they're about to come," he growled, his words sending a shiver of humiliation down my spine.

I couldn't hold back the inevitable any longer. With a strangled cry, my body convulsed in climax, every muscle seizing up as the vibrator drove me over the edge. My vision blurred, and I screamed, the sound raw and broken as it tore from my throat.

"Listen to her fucking scream!" a man shouted. "Slut loves getting her ass wrecked!"

Another voice joined in, jeering and crude. "Bet she wishes she could come like that all the time. Look at her fucking go!"

Degrading comments rained down on me as I shuddered through the orgasm, my body betraying me completely. The doctor pounded into me even harder now that my muscles were choking around him. Then as quickly as he had punched in, he pulled out, leaving me gasping at the sudden emptiness. The relief was fleeting as the burning stretch from the brutal fucking took over, and my body trembled uncontrollably.

"Look at her gaping hole," someone marveled. "Think I can get my fist in there?" The question was almost rhetorical, dripping with cruel curiosity.

The man stepped up to me and slid his fingers over my abused rim, slick with lube. He started with his fingers, pushing several inside me with a sickening ease that made my stomach churn. My body tensed involuntarily, muscles clenching around the intruding digits.

"Fuck yeah," he muttered under his breath. "This slut is gonna take it all."

I couldn't see what was happening behind me, my head hanging down in exhaustion and humiliation. But I could feel everything—the relentless stretch as he worked his fingers deeper into my ass, twisting and curling them to open me up even more.

He added another finger, his knuckles pushing against

my rim as he forced them inside. I cried out at the intense pressure, my body stretched to its limits.

"Come on, you can do better than that," one taunted. "Fucking scream for it! Beg for that fist!"

"Please," I whimpered, the word barely more than a breath. "Please…" I wasn't even sure what I was begging for anymore.

My plea only made them laugh. "You heard her," another man snarled. "She's *begging* for it!"

The man behind me worked his fingers with ruthless determination, forcing them deeper and twisting them inside my stretched ass. Tears streamed down my face as he added his thumb, pushing against the tight ring of muscle with unrelenting pressure.

"Relax, slut," he hissed. "Take this fucking fist."

With one brutal shove, he drove his entire hand past my resisting muscles and into my ass as I screamed in agony. My vision went white with pain as my body spasmed.

"Holy shit," someone breathed in awe. "Look at that! She's taking it all!"

He started moving his hand inside me, slow at first but then faster, pumping in and out with a sickening squelch. Finally, he eased his hand out, and I released the air in my chest with a low groan.

"Wonder what she'd look like with all her holes filled."

A cruel chuckle rippled through the group.

"Let's find out," another voice suggested eagerly.

I barely registered what was happening as they released the restraints binding my wrists and ankles. My body slumped forward, too weak and exhausted to hold myself up. Two pairs of rough hands caught me before I fell, dragging me to the center of the room.

"Look at that," one of them sneered. "Fucking spent already." He slapped my face lightly, making my eyes flutter open just enough to see all their leering faces before someone yanked my head back by my hair.

My body was pliant in their hands, every muscle twitching uncontrollably from overstimulation. It didn't matter to them—they seemed to like it better this way. Someone's fingers dug into my hips as they positioned me on all fours, spreading my legs wide over an eager man's naked lap.

He grabbed my hips and forced me onto his cock, spearing me open with one brutal thrust.

"Fuck, she's dripping," he groaned as he buried himself inside me. His hands roamed over my body, groping and squeezing roughly. "You like that, slut? Fucking moan for me."

That wasn't difficult since the angle rubbed my clit with every thrust. My muscles tightened around his cock as my sighs and moans and pants filled the air.

Another man stepped in front of me, gripping his cock and rubbing it across my face, my mouth. "Open up, whore," he ordered.

I parted my lips just enough for him to shove his cock inside, pushing it deep into my throat until I gagged. He laughed as he grabbed the back of my head and started ruthlessly fucking my mouth.

Behind me, another man spread my ass cheeks wide and pressed the length of his cock against my rim. "Think her ass is still tight after taking a fist?" he jeered.

"Only one way to find out," someone else responded with a dark chuckle.

He drove himself deep into me in one brutal thrust. My entire frame shook as my body was stretched and abused. The wet slap of skin against skin filled the air, mingling with their harsh grunts and curses.

I was impaled on three cocks, every inch of me filled and stretched. The sensations were overwhelming, each thrust sending jolts of pain and pleasure through my body. My muscles spasmed uncontrollably around the invaders, eliciting groans and taunts from the men surrounding me.

"Fuck! How is she still tight?" the man in my ass grunted as he picked up his brutal pace.

"She's loving this," the one fucking my mouth sneered, his voice strained with arousal. "Listen to her moan around my cock."

My muffled cries only seemed to spur them on. The man beneath me thrust up into my pussy with relentless force, grinding against my swollen clit with every movement. Another orgasm was building inside me, making me gasp and writhe even more.

"Come on, slut," he growled through clenched teeth. "Fucking come for us."

They fucked me hard and fast, their cocks pistoning in and out of my abused holes without mercy.

"Bet she's never been fucked like this before," one of them jeered. "Bet no one ever used her like a fucking toy."

The degrading words sent another wave of humiliation over me, but the rising tide of forced pleasure quickly drowned it out. My body reacted against my will, tightening and spasming around the thick invaders stretching me open.

It was too much. The relentless pounding, the brutal stretch of my muscles, the degrading taunts—it all melded into one overwhelming tidal wave of sensation. The orgasm crashed over me like a violent storm. My body convulsed uncontrollably as every muscle seized up in climax.

My cry was swallowed by the cock thrusting deep into my throat, but it didn't matter. They could see my body trembling and quaking, my eyes rolling back as my fingers dug into anything I could grab on to. They heard my ragged gasps and moans escaping around the brutal face-fucking.

"Holy shit, she's coming again!" one of them shouted triumphantly.

"Listen to her fucking scream," another added. "Slut loves getting wrecked!"

The orgasm seemed endless. I pulsed around their cocks, every nerve ending alight.

And they didn't stop.

They didn't even slow down or give me a moment to recover. If anything, my climax only spurred them on, pushing them to new heights of cruelty and filth.

The man fucking my mouth yanked my hair harder, pulling me onto his cock until I gagged around him. "You hear that, whore? Scream! Show us how much you love getting fucked like a bitch in heat."

The words barely registered. My body was trembling violently, muscles spasming as they struggled to process the relentless assault. Somewhere in the haze of torture and ecstasy, I felt hands grabbing at me—fingers pinching my nipples viciously, hands slapping my ass and thighs with stinging force. Voices blended into a cacophony of filthy words and degrading taunts.

"Fucking scream for us!"

"Bet you love getting ruined like this."

"Goddamn slut is dripping everywhere."

"Look at her fucking take it."

"This is what she was fucking made for!"

Suddenly, a switch flipped, and the sensations bombarding me from every direction dulled into an almost serene numbness. It was as if I had floated out of my body, rising above to observe the scene below with detached curiosity. The pain, the pleasure, the raw physicality of it all became distant echoes in a cavernous void.

I watched as they continued to use me, my body malleable and unresisting beneath their rough hands and thrusting hips. My face was a mask of vacant submission, eyes half-lidded and unseeing. The man in my mouth pulled out briefly, allowing me a gasping breath before he shoved back in with renewed vigor. My lips stretched around his cock without protest, my head bobbing at his command like a cork in water.

The man beneath me squeezed my ass hard, his fingers leaving white-hot imprints on my skin as he drove up into my pussy. Each thrust sent my body rocking forward, but I felt none of it. The man in my ass gripped my shoulders for leverage, yanking me back against him with every stroke. Above it all, I heard their voices—clearer now in my disembodied state—mingling with grunts and the slapping sounds of sweaty flesh.

"Fucking take it, all of it!"

"Going to fill this slut up!"

The cock in my mouth swelled, the man's hips bucking

as he held me tight against him. Hot spurts of his cum shot down my throat, and I swallowed reflexively, the taste and texture barely registering. He pulled out, a string of saliva and semen trailing from my lips as I gasped for air.

My vision blurred. The room tilted.

The man beneath me flipped us over, his cock never leaving my pussy as he laid me on my back. He thrust into me savagely, crushing my clit against his pelvis with each stroke.

I think I came again.

The man who had been in my ass moved to straddle my chest, his cock slick as he stroked it in front of my face.

"Open," he commanded. My mouth hung slack, my eyes unfocused as the ceiling swam above me.

Hands grabbed my cheeks, forcing my head to the side. The man on my chest aimed his cock at my face just as he exploded, thick streams of cum splattering across my lips, my cheek, and into my hair. My skin tingled with warmth, but the sensation was fleeting, like a distant memory fading. He sighed with satisfaction as he smeared the remnants across my face with the tip of his cock.

The edges of the room grew dark as my vision tunneled, and the sounds around me muted as if I were sinking underwater.

The man in my pussy was the last thing I saw clearly. His face contorted with lust as he drove into me one final time, his body tensing and then releasing. Hot waves of his cum filled me. He collapsed on top of me, his weight crushing the breath from my lungs.

And then everything went black.

surrender

. . .

I WOKE UP DISORIENTED, my body sore and throbbing, and tried to piece together where I was and how I'd gotten there. I was in a bed—the same bed my master had fucked me on the night I arrived. The room swam in and out of focus, and I had no concept of how long I'd been asleep.

As the grogginess gradually cleared, I noticed a long chain clipped to my collar, the other end attached to a metal slat on the headboard. I tugged at it, testing its strength. It held firm.

"You're awake," came a voice from the corner of the room.

I turned my head gingerly, wincing at the pain that radiated through my neck. My master sat in a chair, his posture relaxed, a smile playing at the corners of his lips. How long had he been there?

He rose from the chair and walked over to the bed, looking down at me with an appraising gaze. "You did well," he said, his tone almost gentle. "My friends were very pleased with you."

The memories of the night rushed back in a sickening wave—the party, the men, the relentless assault. My body tensed involuntarily, ready to endure whatever new torment he might have in store.

"You performed beautifully," he continued, his words sinking into me like daggers. "It means a lot to me that my friends were satisfied. Your obedience, your…enthusiasm did not go unnoticed."

I said nothing, my throat too raw to speak even if I had the courage.

He reached out, and I couldn't stop my flinch, but his touch was surprisingly tender as he stroked a strand of matted hair from my face. "Did you enjoy sleeping in a bed?" he asked, almost as if he cared about the answer.

I nodded slowly, cautious of where this was leading.

"If you continue to behave well," he said, "you'll earn more privileges like this. Life here doesn't have to be hard, you know. All you need to do is serve as you're meant to."

Serve as I'm meant to. The phrase echoed in my mind with a cold finality. This was my life now. My reality. The fight within me, once a roaring flame, flickered weakly, like a dying ember.

He unclipped the chain from my collar, the sudden freedom almost disorienting. I rubbed at my neck around the collar.

"Go clean up and make yourself presentable for me."

I swung my legs over the side of the bed, testing their strength. They wobbled beneath me as I stood, the ache of last night's ordeal settling into my bones. Slowly, I made my way to the bathroom. The mirror reflected a ghost—a woman with hollow eyes, bruises blooming on her skin like dark flowers, dried streaks of—

I turned on the shower and stepped in before it had a chance to warm. The cold water shocked my body to life, rinsing away the filth and memories with each passing second. My fingers traced the contours of my new reality: the collar, the various marks left by hands and mouths. I scrubbed until my skin felt raw, then let the water cascade over me, hoping it could cleanse more than just my skin.

When I emerged from the bathroom, I found my master sitting on the edge of the bed, completely nude, legs spread, dick erect. His body was lean and sinewy, every muscle defined. I'd never seen him fully naked before.

His cell phone was propped on the nightstand, its camera lens aimed squarely at him.

"Come here," he said.

I walked over cautiously but obediently.

"Kneel."

I dropped to my knees before him.

He dangled the chain in front of my eyes, letting it sway like a pendulum.

I lifted my head to allow him access to the collar. The cold metal clicked into place, and I felt a rush of something —fear, anticipation—as I noticed the length of the chain. It had more slack than I'd realized, enough for me to move freely within a small radius.

"You gave my friends so much last night," he said, his voice carrying a note of reproach. "But you see, I'm feeling somewhat…neglected." He leaned back on his hands, thrusting his pelvis forward, and his cock bobbed with the movement. "You fucked everyone but me."

I swallowed hard, my throat still tender. The

implications of what he was saying sank in slowly, like poison seeping through my veins.

"You need to show me how much you appreciate everything I've done for you," he continued. "Worship it."

My mind floated back to the shower, to the brief illusion of cleanliness and clarity. That was gone now, replaced by the stark reality of his demands. I hesitated, and he noticed.

"Do you not want to please your master?" His tone hardened, the gentleness from earlier evaporating like morning dew.

I opened my mouth and took him in at a languid pace, my tongue swirling around the head before I sucked him deeper, inch by inch.

"That's it," he murmured, his hand resting lightly on the back of my head. "Take your time. Make it good."

He glanced at the camera, likely imagining how the scene would play out on his screen later. My every movement had to be perfect—no halfhearted attempts, no visible resistance. If I was going to survive this, I needed to become what he wanted: a creature of pure submission.

I stroked his shaft in rhythm with my mouth, creating a tight seal as I bobbed up and down. I glanced up at him through wet lashes, giving him the doe-eyed look of a willing supplicant. His breath hitched, satisfaction washing over his features.

"You're learning," he said, almost surprised. "Faster than I thought."

I released him with a soft pop, my hand still working his slick length. "Thank you, Master." I licked along the underside of his cock, kissing the tip before taking him back into my mouth with renewed fervor.

His groan reverberated through the room, a primal sound that seemed to awaken a deeper hunger in him. His muscles tensed under my touch, his body rigid with anticipation and lust.

Before I could take another breath, he yanked me up by my hair, pulling me off my knees and bending me over the edge of the bed. My cheek pressed against the cool fabric of the sheets, my breasts flattening against the mattress as he positioned me to his liking.

"Spread your legs," he commanded.

I did as he asked, spreading them wide and arching my back slightly to offer him better access. The cool air kissed my exposed, tender skin, making me shiver.

He grabbed the chain, wrapped it around his fist, and gave it a sharp tug. The collar bit into my neck as he pulled me closer to him.

"You look so fucking perfect like this," he growled. "Like you were made for it."

The head of his cock teased me for a moment before he drove into me with one powerful thrust. I gasped, clutching the sheets as he filled me completely. His pace was relentless from the start, each motion sending jolts of pleasure mingled with pain through my core.

"You take me so well," he groaned, his hands gripping my hips with bruising force. "Such a fucking perfect slave."

Each thrust drove me further into the bed, his cock splitting me with brutal precision.

"So tight." He panted. "So fucking tight after all those men. You're fucking perfect."

His words washed over me in waves, a toxic mix of praise and degradation that left me numb. He was building to his climax, his breathing more ragged, his thrusts losing their rhythm. I braced for the end, for the moment when he'd spill into me and leave me empty and used.

He let go of the chain, and his hands moved to my back as he leaned over me. The sudden release of tension around my neck sent a rush of blood to my head, and with it came a dangerous clarity.

His hot breath was on my ear now, his words a fevered whisper. "You're mine." Thrust. "Fucking mine." Thrust. "Don't you ever fucking forget it."

He slammed into me with one final, violent thrust. His body tensed and then convulsed as he spilled himself inside me. A guttural moan escaped his lips, mingling with his ragged breaths. He held me there for a moment, his cock still twitching, before collapsing on top of me. His weight crushed me into the mattress.

The chain lay coiled in front of my face like a serpent, its cold links reflecting tiny shards of light. My hand moved almost of its own accord, fingers closing around the metal with a grip born of desperation. His sweat-soaked skin pressed against mine, his breath hot and uneven on my neck.

I had no time to lose.

With a swift motion, I wrapped the chain around his neck twice, pulling it tight with every ounce of strength I had left. His eyes shot open in shock and confusion as he clawed at the makeshift garrote.

I wiggled out from under him, using my entire body to yank on the chain. He flailed, trying to dislodge me, but I held fast. He reached for me, then jerked his hands back to the chain, then again to me in a frantic dance of survival.

"Please," he choked out, the word barely audible through his constricted airway.

I put all my weight into the chain, leaning back and bracing my feet against the bed frame. His body convulsed, like a fish pulled from the water, every muscle straining in a last-ditch effort to survive. His flailing grew more desperate, his hands weakly swatting at me, then at the air, before dropping to his sides. His face turned a mottled shade of purple. Veins bulged from his temples and forehead. His sounds were animalistic—a grotesque symphony of wheezes and gurgles.

"Please," he mouthed again, but it was beyond hearing, and I was beyond caring. Each second stretched into an eternity as I watched the life drain from his eyes. This was my only chance, my last bit of control in a world that had ripped it away.

His body convulsed once more, then went limp.

My heart pounded a savage rhythm, each beat echoing in my ears like a war drum. I was past the point of fear, driven by a cold, calculating need to finish what I'd started. If he lived, I was dead—or worse.

A bluish tint spread across his lips and cheeks as oxygen drained from his body.

I didn't let go.

His fingers turned gray.

I didn't let go.

I counted the seconds in my head, each stretching into an eternity. Ten…twenty…thirty…

His chest no longer rose and fell with breath. His hollow eyes stared out, glassy and vacant.

Still, I held the chain tight.

A minute passed. Then another. My hands were numb. My arms trembled with fatigue. I released the chain slowly, cautiously, as if he might spring to life and overpower me.

He didn't.

I thought I would feel something. Relief, remorse, glee, grief, *anything*. But all I felt was cold and numb.

I uncurled my fingers from the chain. The metal links had left deep red imprints on my palms.

My gaze drifted to the phone perched on the nightstand, the red light around the camera lens still on. Realization struck me like a physical blow: everything had been recorded.

I stared at the camera for a long moment, my mind a yawning void. The evidence was undeniable. The footage was a perfect capture of every second, every act, every last breath he took.

And yet, I felt nothing. No fear of the consequences, no panic about what would come next. Just an empty acceptance.

I navigated the touch screen with a surprising steadiness in my fingers as I deleted the video.

A message popped up: "Are you sure?"

I pressed "Yes" without hesitation. It was gone now, but I knew better. The data was still there, lurking in the depths of the device's memory, waiting to be unearthed by someone who knew how.

None of it mattered.

I'd rather go to prison than spend another second under his control.

I absently fingered my collar when another realization struck me. The collar had a tracking device. I remembered my master showing me the app with my tracked location. I could get out of here if I could figure out where I was.

The screen went black before I could do anything else on the phone.

Damn!

I tried to unlock the device to no avail.

Damn! Damn! Damn!

I clicked the only option available for me—an SOS call.

"9-1-1, what's your emergency?" The voice on the other end was calm, almost soothing.

I opened my mouth to speak, but no words came out. I stared at the body splayed on the bed, his head tilted at an unnatural angle, eyes staring into nothing.

"Hello? Can you hear me?"

"I—" My voice cracked. "I need help."

There was a pause, the kind that stretches longer than it should and bends time around it. "Ma'am, are you in immediate danger?"

I clutched the phone tighter, my knuckles white. "Yes. I mean, no...not anymore."

The dispatcher took a slow breath. "Where are you right now?"

"I have no idea. I was brought here two days ago...I think. Maybe three. I don't know where I am, but I need help. Please get me out of here," I begged. Tears welled in my eyes, but they didn't fall. I was too dry, too spent. The fear and the pain had wrung me out like an old dishrag.

"Ma'am," the dispatcher said, cutting through my thoughts like a warm knife through butter. "I've got someone working to trace the call. Stay on the line."

"Okay." My voice was minuscule. I sat on the carpet at the foot of the bed, brought my knees to my chest, and hugged them tightly.

"Can you describe your surroundings?" the dispatcher

asked. "Anything that might help us locate you more quickly?"

I looked around the room. "Not really. There aren't any windows. Nothing with an address. I'm locked in here…"

"Is there anyone with you?"

I looked at my captor's lifeless body. "No. Not anymore."

"Do you know what kind of building you're in?"

"It's a house, I think. A big one. Lots of rooms. Huge. Ostentatious." My voice trailed off as I thought about the gaudy decor, the gold leaf accents, the expensive art on the walls. None of it mattered to me now. None of it even registered.

"We're doing our best to locate you," the dispatcher said. "Help is on the way. Can you tell me your name?"

I hesitated. My name. It seemed like such a small, unimportant thing now, like a toy I'd outgrown. But it was all I had left.

"My name is J—"

The phone was yanked from my hand.

arise

. . .

THE DOCTOR STOOD OVER ME, a gun in his hand, its barrel pointed directly at my head. He was tall and gaunt, his piercing blue eyes seeming to look right through me. His gray toupee was slickly combed over and glistened under the light. His face was a mask of cold, clinical detachment.

He clicked off the call and powered the phone down. "Resourceful," he said, his voice devoid of warmth or emotion.

The phone clattered to the ground. He shot it twice.

I stared up at him, paralyzed with fear. My mind raced, trying to calculate whether I could survive a bullet at this range, whether the sound would alert anyone nearby, whether I could somehow disarm him before he pulled the trigger. The answers came quickly and brutally—no, no, and absolutely not.

"He was livestreaming your performance for me," the doctor said, his voice as cold as the metal he held. "I saw everything."

I glanced at the lifeless body on the bed, my throat constricting with a dread so deep it threatened to consume me whole.

"What…what are you going to do?" I managed to whisper, my voice small and broken.

The doctor's eyes were devoid of human warmth as he regarded me. "I'll miss him," he said, looking at his dead friend with something that might have been affection if he were capable of such an emotion. "But…finders keepers."

It hit me like a speeding car—life was about to get a million times worse. My captor had been sick and twisted, but the doctor was something else entirely. He was perverse. He was pure evil.

He knelt down beside me, the gun dangling in his grip like a child's toy. "You have a choice now. You can come with me willingly, or I can drug you and take you back to my place unconscious. Either way, you're mine," the doctor finished, standing up slowly.

I swallowed hard, my mouth as dry as sandpaper. Every part of me wanted to scream, to fight, to run, but I knew it was useless.

"Please," I said, my voice cracking with desperation. "Just kill me."

The doctor laughed, a short bark that sent chills down my spine. "Kill you? Don't be ridiculous. I'm not into necrophilia."

A wave of nausea washed over me.

"You're a valuable asset," he continued. "At least your cunt is. It would be incredibly wasteful to dispose of you. All you have to do for me is exactly what you would do for your boyfriend." He adjusted himself. "Just a lot better and far more often." He looked at the corpse on the bed. "And if you thought he was rough on you…" He grabbed a fistful of my hair. "You don't know what rough is."

Tears welled up in my eyes, and this time they fell. I couldn't stop them. They poured down my face in hot, wet streams as sobs racked my body. Hopelessness hit me like a sledgehammer, breaking me into pieces. I'd thought it was terrible before, but this…this was a nightmare from which I would never wake.

The doctor grinned, showing too many teeth.

He grabbed me by the hair, yanking me to my feet with a painful jerk. The gun was still in his hand, its barrel now pressed against my temple. The cold metal felt like it was burning into my skin.

"That's right," he sneered, his voice laced with sadistic glee. "Cry for me. Cry like the little bitch you are."

I couldn't help it. The fear and despair were overwhelming. My sobs grew louder, uncontrollable gasps that shook my entire body.

With a sudden, violent motion, he shoved me back onto the bed next to the corpse of my former master. I landed awkwardly, my limbs splayed, and I was disoriented for a moment. The doctor wasted no time. He grabbed my legs and pushed them up over my head, painfully bending me in half. His eyes glinted with malevolence as he stared down at me.

"Keep them there," he ordered, his voice a low, menacing growl.

My whole body trembled as I forced my legs to stay in that unnatural position. He pressed the cold barrel of the gun against my temple again, its icy touch rooting me to the spot with fear. With his other hand, he undid his belt and pants, and they dropped to the floor around his ankles.

"You know what I want," he said, his voice dripping with cruelty. "Give up that pussy like a good slut."

I squeezed my eyes shut, trying to brace myself for what was coming. He'd fucked me before, so I thought I knew what to expect. But nothing could have prepared me for the brutality that followed. He thrust into me without warning, tearing a scream from my throat. The pain was immediate and excruciating.

His movements were violent, each thrust deep and punishing. He leaned in close, his breath hot and foul against my face. "You're mine now," he hissed.

Then he began to fuck me in earnest with all the cruelty and brutality I feared. Each thrust was like a hammer blow, deep and merciless. The pain was searing, like he was ripping me apart from the inside out. Fresh tears streamed down my cheeks as I screamed—high-pitched and broken, my cries reverberating off the walls.

"That's it," he growled as he rammed into me over and over again. "Scream for me, you fucking slut. Scream like the useless whore you are."

I cried out again, the noise torn from my throat by the sheer force of his assault. My body was already sore and tender from the violent gang bang at my master's party. Every inch of me screamed in agony. His relentless pounding made everything infinitely worse. Each brutal thrust sent fresh waves of torment crashing through me. Being set on fire would have been preferable to this hell.

"You like that, don't you? You fucking love it, you worthless whore." He held the gun to my face, its barrel inches from my nose. "Fuck me like your life depends on it…because it does."

I was beyond broken.

Beyond hope.

My body moved on its own, trying to comply with his demands, but every motion sent shards of pain through me. I was a puppet with cut strings, flailing uselessly in his hands.

"That's more like it," he growled, his breath coming in short, ragged bursts. "You're getting the hang of it. This cunt finally knows what it was made for."

The door burst open with a deafening crash, and the room flooded with flashes of shiny black and navy blue.

"Police! Drop the weapon!" The authoritative shout cut through the room like a knife.

The doctor froze mid-thrust, his head snapping toward the sound. I barely registered what was happening, my mind a blurry haze of pain and fear. Several uniformed officers stormed into the room. They fanned out, creating a perimeter around the room, weapons drawn and aimed directly at us.

"Drop it now!" the lead officer barked, his voice leaving no room for negotiation. He was tall and muscular, with soft green eyes that seemed out of place in such a hard, angular face.

The doctor hesitated, his grip tightening on the gun. Time seemed to stretch and warp for a moment, each second an eternity. The tension in the air crackled like static—the kind that comes just before a violent thunderstorm.

For a moment, everything was painfully still. The doctor's piercing blue eyes flicked toward the intruders, calculating and cold. He didn't move to drop the gun. Instead, he gripped it tighter and pressed it firmly to my forehead. The cold steel bit into my skin.

"Last chance!" The lead officer's voice was steady. His stance indicated he was ready for anything.

My mind struggled to process a thousand questions. Had the 9-1-1 operator sent them? Were they able to track my location? Was I saved? Was I going to prison? Would they shoot him? Would he shoot me first?

Then everything happened at once.

Two sharp cracks split the air as the lead officer fired his weapon. The sounds were like whiplashes, painfully loud in the confined space. The doctor's body jerked violently twice, as if struck by an invisible sledgehammer. A look of stunned surprise flashed across his gaunt face, quickly replaced by a sick smile. He tilted back, his legs wobbling, then collapsed forward, his weight crashing down on top of me. The gun slipped from his hand and clattered to the floor.

I was pinned beneath him, his blood leaking onto my body, mixing with my sweat. The metallic tang made me gag. I was too stunned to move, too shocked to even breathe.

"Is she okay?" a voice shouted over the sudden commotion.

The lead officer stepped forward, his weapon still trained on the doctor's lifeless body. "Ma'am," he said, his voice softer now but still carrying the authority of someone used to being in charge. "Are you hurt?"

I stared at him, unable to process the question. *Was I hurt?* The pain in my body was so vast and all-encompassing that it had melded into something unrecognizable, a constant background noise of agony. Hurt seemed too small a word.

He repeated himself. "Ma'am, are you okay?"

I opened my mouth to speak, but no words came out. How could I explain what had happened to me? What was still happening in my mind?

"Clear the house," he ordered his team. The cluster of police officers moved quickly, filing into the hallway, their heavy footsteps receding into the distance. He turned to a man beside him, presumably his partner. "Stay with me, Ross."

The lead officer holstered his weapon and stepped closer to the bed where I lay, still pinned under the doctor's corpse. He moved cautiously, almost tenderly, like someone approaching a wounded animal.

"You're safe now," he said softly. "No one is going to hurt you."

He placed two fingers on the side of the doctor's neck, presumably feeling for a pulse. After a few moments, he carefully rolled the doctor's body off me. The sudden release of pressure made my entire body ache even more intensely, if that was possible.

"Can you sit up?" he asked.

I nodded, then willed my limbs to obey me. Every motion was a new torture as I slowly pulled myself into a sitting position. My eyes were swollen from crying, my vision blurry, but I could still see the concern etched on the officer's face.

He turned back to his partner. "Once the house is clear, get EMS in here." He glanced over at my dead master and checked him for a pulse. "One live victim, two deceased." The officer looked back at me as the partner walked off, chattering into his radio. "Do you have any clean clothes I can grab for you?"

I shook my head, pulling my knees up to cover my body.

"Okay, no problem. EMS will be here in just a minute, and they'll have a blanket you can wrap up in. You're safe now." He looked around the room, his eyes widening as he took in the grotesque pieces of furniture littered with cuffs and restraints.

The officer took a step closer to me, and I cowered away. Now that he had seen what this room, this house… what *I* was for, he was bound to take his turn.

Not again. Not again. Not again.

The partner returned, along with two more officers.

Not again. Not again. Not again.

I crumpled in on myself and desperately hugged my knees tighter to my chest.

"No, please…" I whimpered.

The officer stopped in his tracks, as if reading my fear like an open book. "I'm not going to hurt you," he said, the softness in his voice returning. He waved the other officers back. "No one is going to hurt you. I promise." He held his hands up so I could see his empty palms. He took a tentative step toward me and said gently, "I'm going to remove that collar and chain so we can get you out of here. Is that okay?"

I hesitated, then gave a slight nod. He reached out slowly, making sure not to startle me, and unfastened the leather strap around my neck. It had chafed my skin raw, and the relief was immediate, though the rest of my body still screamed in silent protest.

"I'm Officer Salazar. What's your name?"

I opened my mouth to answer, but nothing fell from my lips.

"Can you tell me what happened?" he asked. His green eyes met mine, and for a moment, I thought I saw something deeper there—an understanding, perhaps, or a recognition of the kind of pain I was in.

I tried to speak, to form the words that would make him understand, but they came out as a jumbled mess. "He…I… The chain…the gun… I didn't…"

Salazar held up a hand to stop me. "It's okay. Let's take it one step at a time." He paused, as if choosing his words carefully. "Are you here against your will?"

I nodded slowly, the cautious movement sending another wave of dizziness through me.

"Are you hurt?"

I hesitated at the woefully inadequate word. I nodded again, even more slowly this time.

His face tightened, and I could see the conflict within him—professional detachment battling with human compassion. "EMS will be here any minute," he said. "They'll take care of you."

I held out my wrists to him, the skin around them bruised and tender. "Are you going to arrest me?"

Salazar looked genuinely confused. "Why would I do that?"

I glanced over at the bed where my master—former captor—lay. He was staring up sightlessly at the ceiling, the chain marks around his neck like a gaudy chunky beaded necklace—the kind my mother used to wear.

Salazar followed my gaze to the lifeless body on the bed, then back to me. His eyes narrowed, not in suspicion, but in contemplation. He shrugged. "I'm not a detective, but that looks like a clear case of autoerotic asphyxiation to me." He took a step back, giving me space. "You're a survivor," he said quietly. "Just hang on a little longer."

A team of paramedics rushed in with a stretcher and medical bags. One of them handed me a blanket, and I wrapped it around my broken body, savoring its scratchy warmth like it was the most precious thing in the world.

One of the paramedics, a woman with deep brown eyes and auburn hair pulled back in a low ponytail, approached me with a stretcher. "Let's get you out of here," she said, her voice a soothing balm to my shredded nerves.

She helped me onto the stretcher with a gentleness that made my body flinch in disbelief. Her touch was careful and respectful, as if she understood the fragility of my current state. She covered me in sheets and warm blankets, layering them over me like protective armor.

"I'm Dayna," she said, her kind eyes meeting mine. "You're going to be okay."

Tears began to stream down my face, hot and relentless. I didn't sob or wail. The tears just flowed, an unstoppable river of relief and exhaustion.

I was safe. Truly safe. From the horrors of the abduction, from the auction house, from the trials, from the ownership, from the rape, from all of it. The realization was too big to hold in my mind all at once. It spilled over, drowning me in its enormity.

Dayna didn't rush me or press for answers. She waited, patient and understanding, as I fought to control my breathing. Each inhale was a battle, each exhale a small victory.

"What's your name?" she asked softly.

I hesitated for a moment.

"Julie," I answered. I was finally free to answer. "My name is Julie."

afterword

You made it through. Well done!

This is the darkest, most unhinged thing I've written to date. (Well…except for that one poem I turned in for a college creative writing class that got me sent to the counselor, but that's a story for another day.)

As I said in the beginning, when I started writing this novella, I had zero intention that it should ever see the light of day. It was a writing exercise for me—the literary equivalent of doodling in the margins. I had a wild, unsettling dream while on vacation with my husband, and I wrote it down as soon as I woke up. (If you're curious, the dream was the "trial" in the first chapter.)

And then I kept writing…

I needed to know what happened to her—what came after she "passed" the trial, after the unspeakable trauma, after her body and will were pushed past the point of breaking. I needed to know if she could survive her captor. If she could overcome him.

That's when I realized what I was really writing: a

heavily fictionalized version of my own trauma. I am a survivor—of sexual assault (twice), a long-term sexually and psychologically abusive relationship, and a near-trafficking experience when I was a young child. (I made it to the trial stage.)

I don't share this to shock you. I share it because these stories matter.

Because silence helps no one.

Because survivors deserve hope and the possibility of an ending where they reclaim their power.

That is why I chose to publish *unnamed*.

resources

If you or someone you know has experienced sexual violence, abuse, or exploitation, please know you are not alone. The following organizations offer confidential support, resources, and guidance for survivors and those who care about them.

Please note: The following resources are based in the United States. If you are located outside the U.S., consider searching online for local organizations and hotlines in your country that support survivors of sexual violence and human trafficking.

RAINN (Rape, Abuse & Incest National Network)

The largest anti-sexual violence organization in the United States. RAINN operates the National Sexual Assault Hotline and provides free, confidential support for survivors of sexual assault.

- Website: www.rainn.org
- National Sexual Assault Hotline: 1-800-656-HOPE (4673)
- Online Chat (24/7): online.rainn.org

National Human Trafficking Hotline

A confidential, toll-free hotline available 24/7 to support victims and survivors of human trafficking, as well as concerned individuals. Trained advocates provide help in more than 200 languages.

- Website: www.humantraffickinghotline.org
- Call: 1-888-373-7888
- Text: "HELP" or "INFO" to 233733 (BEFREE)
- Live Chat: Available on the website

You are not alone. There is help, and there is hope.

acknowledgments

First and foremost, thank you to my husband. You take me with all my scars and baggage—and love me anyway. Because of you, I'm not afraid of the dark anymore. You empower me, emblazon me, and let me bloom into the best version of myself. Thank you for encouraging me to bring this story into the world and talking me out of shelving it when I feared it was too dark. Also, you're a damn good cook.

To my incredible beta readers, ARC readers, and content reviewers: thank you for your thoughtful feedback and for helping me tell the best, most authentic story I can.

To my brilliant editorial and design teams: thank you for breathing life into this project and shaping my chaos into something beautiful.

To my fabulous PA: thank you for keeping my head on straight and being the most enthusiastic cheer squad I could ask for.

To my village—my amazing family and friends: thank you for your unwavering love and support. You've cheered me on, held space for me, and reminded me of who I am when I started to forget. Your belief in me, even in the darkest moments, helped me find the strength to finish this story.

To my readers: every time I write something that resonates with you, my world lights up. Your notes, messages, reviews, and emails mean more than I can say. You make the long nights and vulnerable moments worth it.

During my active-duty military service, I had the privilege of serving as a sexual assault victim advocate and program coordinator. Helping other survivors on their journeys was deeply humbling and a vital part of my own healing. I was fortunate to work alongside some of the most compassionate, talented advocates and counselors. Thank you for your companionship, then and now.

Thank you to my own counselors—for helping me face the dark, drag it into the light, and find my way back to myself.

And to every version of me that came before—the scared little girl, the silenced survivor, the woman who didn't know if she'd ever feel whole again—we made it. You carried me through the fire. This book is for you, too.

thirsty for more?

Check out Nadine's other books!

starcrossed nocturne

An ancient vampire running from her tortured past.

A human mystic who sees the light within her.

A forbidden love could destroy them both…

———

For the most up-to-date listing of works by Nadine Theiss, visit:

www.nadinetheiss.com/books

about the author

This title appears under N. Theiss (read it aloud)—the name Nadine Theiss uses when the stories get darker, sharper, and a little more unhinged. Same author, just with the brakes cut.

———

Nadine Theiss is a U.S. Navy veteran with a sharp pen and a taste for the unexpected. She's been writing since she was twelve—long before she had any idea just how far stories could go. With degrees in Modern Language and Psychology and a passport that's seen some things, she blends rich cultural detail with  emotional depth and just the right amount of bite.

Whether she's crafting fierce heroines, bending genre lines, or burning down outdated expectations, Nadine writes with fearless intensity and without apology. She draws inspiration from *The Great Gatsby*, *Memoirs of a Geisha*, and the deep lore of *Star Trek*, *Star Wars*, and *Harry Potter*.

She lives in Charleston, South Carolina, where she's

fueled by coffee, chaos, and the occasional trivia night—
always chasing the next story that refuses to behave.

————

connect with nadine!

Join the Fan Club for first looks, cover reveals, behind-the-
scenes peeks, upcoming events, and first dibs on books and
promos.

www.nadinetheiss.com

Like the darker side of N. Theiss? Visit her dedicated page
to learn more. (If you dare…)

www.nadinetheiss.com/ntheiss

follow nadine on social!

facebook.com/nadine.theiss.writer
instagram.com/nadine.theiss.writer

www.ingramcontent.com/pod-product-compliance
Lightning Source LLC
Chambersburg PA
CBHW030009010826
48973CB00009B/2736